P9-EMR-408

Sugar's
Daddy

Sugar's Daddy

Kaira Denee

URBAN BOOKS

http://www.urbanbooks.net

This is a work of fiction. Any references or similarities to actual events, real people, living or dead, or to real locales are intended to give the novel a sense of reality. Any similarity in other names, characters, places, and incidents is entirely coincidental.

URBAN SOUL is published by

Urban Books
1199 Straight Path
West Babylon, NY 11704

ISBN-13: 978-1-59983-039-1
ISBN-10: 1-59983-039-6

First Printing: January 2009

10 9 8 7 6 5 4 3 2 1

Printed in the United States of America

Acknowledgments

Writing my second novel was a lot of fun. There were key people that influenced my ideas and writing and I'd like to thank them formally.

Ma—Thanks for everything! There are way too many things to name them specifically here, but you have always given yourself to me unselfishly. Your feedback on *Sugar's Daddy* really restored my confidence.

Shauntane—You always give your honest feedback, and although sometimes I don't listen, believe me . . . I hear you! Thank you.

Marlon—Whenever I need to write, you're always willing to take the kids and give me the space (and quiet) I need to be creative. You always show interest in my plots and try your best to give me ideas. Thanks for your support!

Torrian—Thank you for all your help in promoting *Take It There*. You've proven to be a great business contact and a great friend too. Your words of encouragement definitely kept me going. Thank you in advance (wink) for your help in promoting *Sugar's Daddy*!

Daynel and Jasmin—Thanks to my sisters for giving me yet another reason to *try* to be a good role model. You guys make me proud and I hope I make you proud too!

Nana—You're just the best in every way. I know you always have my back. Thanks for introducing me to some key people that were able to give my book release a boost!

Finally thank YOU for reading my second novel. I hope I can count on your continued support!!

God is good. . . .

Prologue

"Don't leave me," Payton begged Keisha that night.

He didn't realize it at the time, but it would be the last time he'd see his new bride.

Keisha was wearing a red dress. No, not just any ol' red dress. *The* red dress of red dresses. The first time she'd worn the red dress, Keisha gave every man in the room whiplash when she and Payton walked through the door. It hugged her in all the right places but left just enough to the imagination to drive any man wild.

Keisha finally responded after stopping in her tracks and turning to face her husband.

"I won't be out long. Don't worry."

"Don't go," he begged again, now stepping toward her.

It wasn't just the fact that she was going out. Payton was upset because she'd been out every other night for the past month, leaving Payton at home to care for their daughter, Alana.

"Look, Keisha, I'm tired of this shit. I know something's going on and you need to keep it real and tell me something."

Keisha was only a few steps away from the door,

impatiently waiting to get through it. It wasn't that Keisha didn't love her family. She did. She just wasn't ready to take on so much responsibility so soon. In a two-year period she'd had a baby. Been dumped by the baby's father. Met a wonderful man who took the responsibility to help raise her daughter. And now she was married to him. It all just happened too damn fast. Her dreams, her goal of becoming a nurse, had all begun dissipating before her eyes. She was bored with her new life and wondered when and where she'd lost herself along the way.

Payton approached her and grabbed her hand. It was cold and clammy.

"You fucking somebody else?" he asked. The concern in his voice now turned into complete anger.

He doesn't want to know the answer to that, Keisha thought. *The truth would kill him.*

The truth was, there was another man. And he was indeed waiting for Keisha to arrive.

"Why are you disrespecting me like that, Payton?" she whined, pretending to be offended by his accusations.

"Are you fucking somebody else?" Payton asked again, deliberately enunciating his words as he went along.

Keisha turned quickly to leave, but Payton grabbed her arm, and then he quickly drew back. He was astonished at how bony her arm felt. Giving her a once-over, Payton realized that the red dress didn't quite fit her the same anymore. It was damn near hanging off her. It suddenly made sense why she'd begun wearing baggy sweatpants and loose T-shirts to bed. Payton had been working a nine-to-five shift, while Keisha worked part-time at night, so they didn't see that much of each other. And with her going out all the time, they hadn't been intimate in over a month.

The look on his face made Keisha think he'd discovered her secret. *Well, I wasn't hiding it that well,* she reasoned.

Still in shock, Payton asked, "Are you purging again?"

When they'd first met, Keisha had been depressed from being left a single mother, and she had desperately trying to lose her baby weight. She would stick her finger down her throat to force her food back up. Payton discovered it very early on and threatened to break up with her if it didn't stop immediately. She'd quit that habit cold turkey. Actually, stopping the habit was quite easy when she realized that Payton didn't mind the weight; he adored her curves.

Keisha seized the opportunity to make a dramatic exit.

"You promised you would never bring that up again, Payton!" she screamed, and ran out the door.

"Keisha!" he yelled after her but couldn't chase her. Their baby was asleep in her crib.

Four hours later.

Two A.M.

The phone rings.

Wide awake and worried out of his mind, Payton answers with a gruff hello.

Keisha's on the line, whispering something that Payton can barely make out.

"What, Keisha?" he yelled, getting agitated, fully prepared to continue the argument they'd begun hours earlier.

"If I don't come home tonight," he heard, "please promise me you'll take care of my baby. Please?"

Payton swallowed the thick fear that quickly gathered in the back of his throat.

"Promise me, Payton!" she screamed with frightening intensity.

"I promise, but, Keisha, what's wrong? Why are you whispering? What the hell is going on?"

Payton stood up. Helpless. He paced back and forth across the room.

"I gotta go," she continued, still whispering. "Please take care of my baby!"

Payton thought he heard sirens in the background and a man yelling in the distance, but he was straining so hard to hear her, he couldn't be sure.

"Keisha, if you need help, tell me where you are and I'll come get you."

The sirens got louder. Or was it just loud music?

Keisha screamed.

The line went dead.

Chapter 1

Payton

Seventeen Years Later . . .

Summer paced around my bedroom for hours, rehashing the intricate details of our failed love affair. An affair that I was trying to end that night. I told her over and over why we weren't working out. She told me over and over where I needed to improve as a man.

"You don't send me flowers anymore," she hissed.

"You don't deserve 'em."

Her head snapped around and she murdered me with her glare.

"You don't compliment me anymore. You used to always tell me how beautiful I was."

"You don't take care of yourself anymore," I said plainly, resting my elbows on the pillow I'd placed in my lap.

She stood there, mouth agape, with her hands resting on her hips. Her mouth was moving faster than a woodpecker as I began to tune her out.

When I first met Summer, she was a dime. She

was about ten pounds lighter. Kept her hair and nails tight. And the way she dressed was always to impress. Now, don't get me wrong—when I fall in love with someone, those things don't matter. But I wasn't feeling her on that level yet and she'd already started getting too damn comfortable.

Nowadays she's most comfortable in gym sweats with her hair pulled back in a ponytail. So I guess I fell for her representative, not the *real* her. In my experience I've found what women didn't seem to understand about me is that I'm simple. And I know what I like. Let's say I become infatuated with a woman because she has a cute little haircut and keeps her nails elaborately decorated with jewels and all kinda colors. Then she decides to grow her hair out and start getting conservative French manicures, that's on her. They don't understand that when I don't jump on them at every given chance, it's because they took away the little things that drove me crazy to begin with. With that said, the rules change when you fall in love. And like I said, I was not feeling Summer like that.

She's very hard to love. Plus, she grew her hair out after I insisted I love women with short hair. She was also jealous, controlling and very insecure. Mainly, she didn't respect my daughter and our relationship. My daughter, Alana, can be a damn trip herself, but for now she's my number one focus. I promised her mother that I'd take care of her, and that was a promise I will not renege on. And Summer was taking up too much of my time and energy and just becoming way too high-maintenance.

Chapter 2

Cassie

I dismounted Brice and my limp body fell on the bed beside him, my insides still quivering. Covered in sweat, the cool air from the fan made my moist skin tingle. Moisture thickened the air, which labored my breathing. My ears rang. My toes were numb. Heart just a-racing. My breath would soon return to me. But for now we both just lay there, staring at the ceiling.

Ex-sex is the best sex.

"Brice, can you get me a glass of water?" I asked, chest heaving.

He didn't answer. Just sat up, shook his head back and forth, trying to regain his composure. He slid on his boxers and headed out of my room. I noticed him stop halfway down the hallway and peek in on our daughter, Mia. He took a look and kept it moving; she was knocked out. I would soon follow her lead after I guzzled my water. Brice had worn me out! I was in for a good night's sleep, or so I thought.

After about five minutes passed, I got suspicious.

My apartment was only seven hundred square feet—it don't take that damn long to get to the kitchen and back. By that time I felt enough strength and my breathing had returned to normal, so I got up to see what was going on. I stood up and my legs were still shaking. *Damn, Brice,* I thought. Smiling shyly, I thought of the nasty things we'd just done to each other. He knows how to put it down!

Instinctively, as I made my way down the hall, I peeked in on Mia too. She looked like an angel. I could see from there that Brice wasn't in the kitchen. Taking a right at the corner, I noticed light coming from under the door of my half bath off the living room. Then I heard Brice whispering and telling lies. He was telling the person on the other side of the phone that he would be crashing at Chuck's house tonight and he'd see them tomorrow. "A'ight, I love you too. Good night."

Chapter 3

Payton

Yeah, I was being an asshole, but I was fed up with Summer, and no matter what she said that night, our relationship was over. On my terms.

"Look," I interrupted her tirade, "I am tired of all the accusations. I'm tired of you trying to control my life and shift my focus. And I'm tired of you and Alana getting into it all the time. If you can't respect my daughter and the fact that she's been through some shit and needs her father, then you're not the kind of woman I want to be with."

"You're not her father," she spat.

Her slick-ass mouth. Another reason why I didn't want to be with her anymore. She always tried her best to hit below the belt just to win an argument. This time she'd gone way too far.

"You know what, Summer? You can leave. Right now. Get the hell outta my house with that bullshit. I've raised her since she was six months old and I don't give a damn if I didn't fuck her mother to make her. I *am* her father."

"Oh, you're a big man now, cursing at a woman. What a gentleman," she sang mockingly.

"Get out!" I screamed. She had struck the wrong chord with me. "Take all your shit if you ever want to see it again and get the fuck out."

This time she knew I was dead serious. She scurried around my room, grabbing various items from here and there and stuffing them into her oversized Chanel purse . . . which I'd bought her. I felt like snatching it off her shoulder and throwing it *and* her out the window. But I walked away before I did something I'd regret.

"Don't you fucking walk away from me, Payton. We are not done here. How dare you try to kick me outta your house?"

"Just leave!" I yelled, not bothering to turn around. I headed for the door downstairs and opened it up for her.

She flew down the stairs, missing the last step and almost breaking her neck.

Her tone softened and tears were in her voice. "I'm not going anywhere until you give me a good explanation to why you are breaking up with me. I thought you loved me?"

"Look, I'm going to take a drive. Don't be here when I get back," I said, walking out and leaving her in the doorway.

"I'm not leaving, Payton. You will not kick me out like some two-dollar ho."

"OK, well, if you're here when I get back, then I'm calling the police. Don't test me."

I drove off, leaving her in the doorway. Usually,

I would've felt guilty about breaking up with a woman so hard-core. . . . I'm usually quite the gentleman. But Summer crossed the line. And whatever little bit of feelings I had for her were gone immediately when she brought my daughter into it.

Chapter 4

Cassie

OK, now, Brice is my ex-fiancé, and for now my status in his life was merely his baby-mama and he is no more than my baby-daddy and occasional sex partner. But a role I will never play is the other woman. But I damn sure stood outside the bathroom with my arms folded over my naked body, looking like I was the main woman.

"My name is Chuck now?" I asked him after he flushed the toilet and emerged from the bathroom.

"Cassie, look, I've been wanting to talk to you anyway. She ain't nobody to me. I want to talk about us."

"Obviously, she *is* somebody, because you just snuck behind my back to call her and tell her some lie as to your whereabouts. If she was nobody, then she doesn't deserve the courtesy call in the middle of the damn night. Remember the courtesy call that you never bothered to give me when I *was* somebody to you?"

"Aw, here you go. Look, I'm just trying to learn

from the mistakes I made with you and be a better man, Cassie. Which is why I want to talk about us. I want to get back together with you. I want to be a family again! Look at our beautiful daughter. You and her living in this tiny-ass apartment! You and my princess deserve better than this," he yelled, pointing around at my apartment.

"Lower your voice or this conversation is over, Brice. If you wake Mia up, I *will* kill you."

"Can we talk, though? Let's go in the room. I'm serious."

I turned around, feeling silly that I was naked. Feeling like an idiot because here I was angry over this man once again. We could talk all night, but I knew already that I would not be his fool again. I'd leave it for the girl believing the bull he just fed her over the phone.

I angrily snatched a T-shirt out of my drawer and threw it over my head and plopped on my bed, Indian-style, readying myself for a long night. *Why am I the only one that understands our arrangement?* I'd been on a sabbatical from men, and sex with Brice was convenient. Never mind the fact that he knew every crevice of my body, where to lick, where to bite, what to smack, when to slow down, when to speed up . . . the man just knew what to do. I'd get it, when I needed it, just how I liked it. It would be easier than dating around, or so I thought. Our situation had just become more difficult than ever.

I made it very clear that our ex-sex would only continue if he was unattached and I was too. Of course we both planned on moving on to pursue serious relationships, but in the meanwhile we'd continue to enjoy one of the best aspects about our failed four-year relationship, the sex. We agreed that if either of us got involved, we'd tell the other and end our dealings. Since there'd been several other women in our relationship when Brice and I were together, I told him from the jump that I would never be *her*. And here I was . . . the other woman in the flesh.

Every now and then Brice would get all sentimental and want to take a try at our relationship again. I can't even front. After the way we'd just made love, I might have fallen for it that night. Recently he and I'd been getting along better than ever. He's always been a great father to Mia, so that was never an issue. But he'd just broken the rules of our arrangement. And now I wasn't sure how long I'd been the other damn woman! *I'm not having it,* I reminded myself.

Brice sat in front of me, holding my hand for hours, trying to convince me that we needed to get back together. I didn't say much. Just kept reminding him that *he* broke the rules of a very simple arrangement. How could I trust him with a deeper commitment?

It was sad. I'd loved this man for so long and even bore his child, but I knew better. He would never do right by me.

I never did get my water that night. My throat remained dry and became even worse by me swallowing the lumps that kept forming in my throat. We both shed a bucket of tears. It was the first time I saw him cry. Maybe he finally realized, I am stronger now and will not stand for anything less than what I know I deserve.

I stood at the door, watching him walk down the hall to the elevator at four in the morning.

"Brice," I called after him. "I still love you. I just love *me* more."

His eyes locked with mine as the elevator door opened. "Cassie, I love you more than I love myself," he half whispered, walking into the elevator.

Chapter 5

Payton

The next morning when Alana and I were getting in the car, Summer called. I promptly pushed the ignore button and kept it moving through the thick heat. Alana and I were on our way to her therapy session and I had no time for Summer's drama. I decided to just turn the phone off.

Alana resented her therapy sessions, but her principal, Dr. Morton, her aunts and grandmother agreed it was best, considering the circumstances she'd been through. With the exception of Alana's principal, I took the other women's advice with half a grain of salt, though. When Keisha first disappeared, they didn't help me out at all. Unless they wanted to borrow money from me, they weren't around. But being that they were all battling some type of substance abuse, I didn't want them around Alana that much anyway.

Once Alana was old enough to be told the truth—that her mother left her and me—she just couldn't understand how a mother would do such a thing. Alana immediately thought it was her fault or that she just wasn't good enough. She felt if her own mother didn't love her enough, how could anyone else? She began throwing unbelievable tantrums when she didn't get her way and became increasingly violent in school with other children. After beating a boy up with a bat in gym class, Dr. Weinstein prescribed some medication to help balance her moods. I sure hated sneaking into her room after she left for school to count her medication to make sure she was taking them daily. The medicine was not an option, Dr. Weinstein, her therapist insisted; they were mandatory.

It was Alana's senior year of high school and Dr. Weinstein thought that her dosage could be lowered after graduation, and they'd continue to see each other twice a month until she felt Alana was ready to face the world on her own.

We rode in our usual uncomfortable silence on the way up High Ridge Road, one of the longest streets in Stamford that separated the working and middle class from the well-to-do. Alana had her earplugs in, listening to her iPod, ignoring me. Shit, I put on my Anthony Hamilton and tuned her out too. The drama the night before with Summer was still fresh on my mind.

We pulled up to Dr. Weinstein's office five minutes early and Alana rushed inside, not looking back to see if I was behind her or not. I didn't sit in on her sessions anymore. Not since she turned thirteen and girly things started happening to her. She didn't feel too cool with me knowing all her goings-on.

When I made it inside, I caught a glimpse of Alana's back entering the office. She knew I'd be waiting in the lobby when she finished, as always.

I plopped down on the suede love seat, adjacent to Dr. Weinstein's assistant, Molly.

Molly's a cute white girl with a heart-shaped face, small nose and pursed lips. Her eyes were this amazing light green that really stood out against her tanned complexion. Her short hair was jet black and hugged the sides of her childlike chubby cheeks. Molly's appearance stood in stark contrast from Dr. Weinstein's—a petite, frail woman, with pale olive skin, stringy brown hair and a bulbous nose juxtaposed onto her narrow face.

"Good morning, Mr. Harris," she greeted me, always keeping it professional.

"Good morning, Molly," I returned, taking an extra moment to analyze her pretty face and admire her cleavage.

For a fleeting moment, the thought of crossing the color lines to find love ran through my mind. More like sprinted through my mind; the idea was out the door almost as soon as it entered. Shit, no thanks. I'd rather continue trying my hand with the evil I already know . . . *sistas*. I wouldn't let Molly's cute ass or Summer's crazy ass steer me away from my sistas.

I took the rest of my free time to turn my phone back on and check the message Summer left for me. More like messages. The first one started off normal, "Hi, it's me. I hate what happened last night and I'm sorry for the comment I made about Alana. We need to talk. Call me." Second one had sprinkles of fury in its tone. "Hmmm, so it picked up on the first ring this time. Did you turn your phone off? You know what? We really need to talk if you think you have to start disrespecting me like that." Third one . . . "So you really did turn your phone off? You sorry, mutha" . . . and so on. Fourth one . . . "Let me tell you something, Payton. . . ." Fifth one. "I am not the one, you hear me? How dare you . . ."

The anger and insults got progressively worse as I listened to the messages in their entirety and deleted all twelve of them.

My sistas. Gotta love 'em.

The thirteenth message was from my boy Damon, inviting me out to Negril on West Third Street in Manhattan. Damon was sure to get me in trouble; that fool doesn't have any sense. But that's why he's my boy. The things that I'd murmur under my breath, he'd belt out loud and ignorantly. Always the life of the party and dripping with confidence, my boy is that dude in any social gathering that women just gravitate toward. He's handsome, I've been told. The ladies think he looks like Eric Benét, but a shade darker. Looks like a broke-down Teddy Riley with dreads to me, or at least that's what I tell him to bring him back down to earth sometimes. A night out with Damon was sure to get my mind off Summer's trifling ass and on to bigger and better things.

I text-messaged him my reply: Let's roll!

The office was suddenly too damn quiet and my thoughts drifted back to Alana. *Damn, thirty minutes still left,* I thought.

She's no angel, but she's my baby girl. Last night I realized that until she left for college in September, I might as well not even try to have a serious girlfriend. From the beginning Alana hated Summer, giving her the cold shoulder and rejecting any efforts Summer made to make peace. There were a couple of other women that I had had serious relationships with before Summer. When Alana was younger, she pretty much liked anyone I brought around. It was as she got older that she began with the nonsense, but she never behaved this way before. It wasn't until Summer stepped on the scene six months ago that Alana really started with her shit. When Summer started growing her hair out, Alana was the first to comment on how raggedy she looked. Sent Summer running up the stairs crying. At first, Summer tried to be the adult, but she was soon reduced to very childish behavior too. A couple times I had to physically drag Summer away from Alana to avoid a fistfight.

I never have, or will, put any woman before my daughter, but I sure was glad that Alana would soon be off to college. I'm damn near forty and still want more kids one day and a functional relationship with a woman.

I still remember how pissed Damon was when I made the decision to raise Alana instead of giving her to her half-assed aunts or grandmother. Damon had a fit.

You don't owe Keisha shit. Let her family raise her.
I am her family. She calls me Daddy.
No disrespect, but you only been with Keisha for, like, a year.
She's my wife.
How you gonna take care of a little girl?
I'm not running from this responsibility.
It's not your responsibility to run from, man.
Her biological's nowhere to be found, her three aunts have thirteen kids between them and her grandmother is a damn alcoholic.
True . . . And I promised Keisha before we got married that Alana would have the life she never got.
A'ight, then, if you're serious about this, then I got your back.

It was the only time I ever won a debate with Damon. A year later, when I had Alana baptized, I presented Damon with the honor of being her godfather. Surprisingly, he excitedly accepted.

"Mr. Harris," Molly yelled, jarring me from my thoughts. She frantically ran from behind her desk. "Dr. Weinstein needs you in her office. Something's wrong with Alana. Hurry, please!"

Chapter 6

Cassie

When I woke up Saturday morning, drained and dizzy from lack of sleep, I knew this was it. We were finally over; the end of an era. And it was on my terms. Brice, I'm sure, would still be a major part of Mia's life, but he and I were officially "black history."

From the faint whisper of Saturday-morning cartoons coming from her room, I knew Mia was up. Before saying good morning to my angel, I freshened up a bit; swishing some mouthwash around in my mouth, washing my face and hand-combing my hair until I looked halfway decent.

"Good morning, honey," I sang, entering her Maya + Miguel–themed room. "Maya + Miguel" is her favorite TV show.

"Good morning, Mommy. Can I have some cereal? I'm hungry."

"Sure, babe," I said, taking a seat beside her on the bed and rubbing her extra thick, cottony head of hair.

"Mommy," she said, voice sounding a bit more stern, almost like she was reprimanding me.

"OK, OK, I'm going. You want Healthy O's or Sugar Loops?" I asked teasingly, knowing damn well she didn't want anything with the word "healthy" in it.

She cracked up, though. "You're silly, Mommy."

After breakfast we dressed; Mia in her karate gi and me in my sweats and headed to her weekly lesson at the Y. Her lessons gave me an hour to run errands and gave Mia the opportunity to exercise and learn some discipline. It was a win-win situation.

As usual, we met up with Tasha, my best friend, and her five-year-old daughter, Freesia, in the lobby before heading upstairs to the gym.

"Uh-huh," Tasha remarked, noticing my sullen demeanor.

I smirked back, letting her know once the kids were gone, I had a story to tell.

"OK, girls. You have a good time and listen to Sensei Brian!" I yelled after them as they snatched off their sneakers and socks and ran into formation. They were getting so big, I noticed with a longing glance.

Tasha's situation was much different from mine. There was no lingering baby-daddy, no drama, no nothing. He has nothing to do with her or Freesia. Tasha had been the other woman in her situation, believing that one day Keith would leave his wife and be with her. But once she got knocked up, it must've knocked some sense into Keith. He suddenly remembered his vows, begging Tasha to have an abortion because he could no longer continue the adultery. Tasha pondered it. After all, it wouldn't have been her first abortion. But in the end she decided against it, and decided to show up at Keith's door to tell his wife about their affair and the child they were expecting together. But when Keith's wife answered the door, looking like she was due to drop her own baby any day, and looking just as beautiful as she wanted to look, Tasha changed her mind, pretending to be at the wrong address.

Being that I was pregnant at that time too, I encouraged her to own up to her responsibilities and keep the baby. We did it together, and Freesia was born three months after Mia.

We left the Y, crossing Washington Boulevard, and headed to the nail shop across the street to get our tips filled in. It was early, so all the teenage girls hadn't invaded that shop yet, and we were able to get right in. Tasha took a seat to my right and dived right into my business.

"So why you out here looking like who did it and forgot to finish?" she quipped.

"Fun-ny," I replied, rolling my neck. "Anyways, Brice was over last night."

"Girl, I know you're not still fucking him. When are you going to stop letting him use you like that?"

"He's not using me, Tasha. It's a mutual agreement we have . . . well, had."

"Mutual arrangement, huh?" she said sarcastically. "Whatever helps you sleep at night, honey. What color you getting?"

"Yeah, whatever. I think I'ma get this one," I said, passing her the bottle of pearly pink polish. "But please tell me why . . . he snuck off into my bathroom and was telling some chick that he was spending the night at Chuck's house tonight, and before he hung, up he told her he loves her."

"Mmm . . . how is Chuck's fine ass anyway?" Tasha asked dreamily, giving the nail polish back to me. "That's too light. Pass me that red one on the bottom row."

"Stay focused, Tasha. Anyways, then he wants to get all lovey-dovey and talkin' about he wants us to get back together and so on. But I'm not going to fall for it this time. I've been through too much with him. He is not going to waste my best years."

"Well, do you think he's serious?"

"Of course he's serious. I know he loves me. But he only loves me the best he can, and that's just not good enough anymore. He's just not a one-woman man, and maybe some other chick will be OK with that, but not me."

"OK, so no more ex-sex then, right?"

Lee, my manicurist, interrupted to ask if I wanted a trim. I nodded yes in response.

"No. I'm through with him. We can deal for Mia's sake and that's it."

"You pay now," Lee said, interrupting again.

"I hope you mean it this time, because you guys have been carrying on like this since forever. I got you. Don't worry about it," she said, digging into her purse for money. "What you need is to meet someone new."

"Tell me about it. But where? Who? I never go anywhere but to the grocery store, the Y, your house and here. Thanks, girl, I'll pay next time."

"Exactly. So let's go out. Tonight."

"And who's going to babysit the girls?"

"I got you covered. Last week I saw this advertisement at the cleaners for this high-school girl that'll babysit for ten dollars an hour. I used her the other day when I had to pick up Shauny from the airport late night, remember?"

"Oh, yeah, and Mia and I both had that stomach bug."

"Yeah. She's a sista, college bound, Freesia loved her. My house was clean when I got back and she was awake doing homework and Free was knocked out."

"All right, cool. Where're we going?"

"I'll get back to you on that, but it's on. We haven't been out in a minute, though. I can't wait."

We both went to the back to wash our hands and get ready for our polishing; then we returned to our seats.

"I'll check my e-mail when I get home. You know I always get those party notifications and e-flyers clogging up my mailbox," Tasha suggested.

"Yeah, I know, and you always forward 'em to me and clog up my damn mailbox."

After our manicures were dry, we picked up the girls from the Y and headed our separate ways, agreeing to speak later about where'd we go for the night.

On the way home I told Mia that she'd have a sleepover at Freesia's tonight and that a nice girl would be babysitting them.

"What's her name, Mommy?" Mia asked about the babysitter.

"Actually, baby, I don't know."

"She's a stranger?"

"Not really a stranger, because Auntie Tasha has met her and she babysat Freesia. Freesia had a good time with her and she's really nice," I tried, assuring her.

"I want to go to my daddy's house."

"Why, baby? Freesia is going to be sad that you're not going to her house."

"Because I want to see my daddy. He's sad. I heard him crying last night. You were crying too."

My heart folded over.

"I thought you were sleeping?"

"I heard it when I went to the bathroom. Then I got back in the bed."

"We can call him when we get home, OK?"

I wondered how much of our argument she'd heard, and if she understood any of it. When he and I first separated, she was so young she didn't quite grasp it all, and we didn't bother sitting her down for a talk. It was too confusing for her little brain to process. But now she knows something's awry, and I never wanted her to be aware of our problems.

Chapter 7

Payton

I charged into the doctor's office to find Alana hoisting a star-shaped paperweight behind her, preparing to throw it at Dr. Weinstein.

"Alana!" I yelled, running toward her and grabbing her arm.

"I don't know what happened. She just lost it!" Dr. Weinstein screamed, looking scared for her life.

"What the hell is wrong with you, girl?" I spat, jerking Alana by her wrist and freeing the paperweight from her clenched hand. "Sit down!"

Alana's face was flooded with tears, nostrils flared and lips quivering. She wouldn't talk, just sat there in a daze.

Dr. Weinstein's chest was heaving and she held her right hand over her heart.

"She already lodged this at me," she said, holding up her stapler. "Good thing I ducked."

"What happened in here, Doctor?"

Dr. Weinstein finally took her seat and snapped back into a professional demeanor, surprisingly fast.

"Mr. Harris, Alana and I were discussing her social life—friends, what she's been doing in her spare time. Then I asked how she and Parker were doing. Everything was fine up until that point. When I asked about Parker, she stared at the floor for the longest. When she looked up, tears were in her eyes and then she just flew into a rage, telling me that I'm crossing the line, getting too far into her business—"

"I'm sorry, Dr. Weinstein," Alana interrupted, almost robotically. "I don't know what got into me. It's just that Parker and I have been going through some issues lately. I didn't mean to lash out at you. My anger was misguided. I apologize."

Dr. Weinstein gave me a brief look of concern before responding. "I accept your apology, Alana. So you're feeling better now?"

"Yes, Dr. Weinstein. Again, I apologize. You're one of my best friends. I can't believe I did that." Alana shook her head, then smiled angelically.

I sat there dumbfounded, disbelieving all that I had just witnessed. I saw Alana damn near spitting fire out of her nose, and a minute later she was sweet as pie. *What the hell?* I just kept my mouth shut, sure that Dr. Weinstein knew better how to handle this situation.

"Alana," Dr. Weinstein spoke slowly, "let's end here for today. Maybe next week you'll be ready to tell me what's going on with you and Parker. I'd like to help you get through it. Right now, though, I'd just like to have a quick word with your dad, alone."

"Sure," she replied excitedly. "Daddy, I'm just going to run across the street and get some gum. Then I'll meet you back in the waiting room." She kissed my cheek and walked out.

"Since this is supposed to be group therapy anyway, I don't feel it's a problem to share my concerns with Alana. I think I need to change her medication. She needs something a little stronger. Now that she's in a relationship, she's dealing with a lot of new emotions. I think she needs help coping with them. I mean, as you know, she's had outbursts in the past, but never a violent one like this. We need to nip this in the bud, because if she tries lashing out on someone else like this, she might get hurt, or she might end up seriously hurting someone."

"Should I talk to her? Reprimand her when we get home? What should I do?" I felt helpless.

"Just leave it alone for now. See, Alana's extremely intelligent. She realizes what she did here today was unacceptable. The last thing we want is for her to feel that you are disappointed with her. You know she thinks the world of you."

"OK," I agreed.

"I'm writing you a prescription for Geodon. It might give her headaches at first but should really help in maintaining her bipolar disorder. Remember, although Alana is usually in the manic state of happiness, her depressive states are very low and violent. We want her to be able to maintain a healthy amount of both emotions. Bipolar disorder is a lifelong disease, but with counseling and the proper medication, she will live a happy and healthy life. Many people do, you know? Just try your best to exercise more patience when dealing with her, OK?"

It wasn't like she was telling me something that I didn't already know, but I guess since I was so freaked out, she felt the need to calm me down.

"But I have one more concern," Dr Weinstein informed me while I was still distracted with my thoughts.

"Lay it on me." I heaved a sigh.

"I think she might be sexually active with Parker. As you know, sexual relationships bring on a strong wave of emotions, especially in teenage girls. Do you mind if I talk to her about that and recommend she see a gynecologist to get her on birth control?"

"Oh, Jesus. I'm going to have a heart attack today," I replied. *Hell no, I don't want you to talk to her about sex,* I thought. *I don't even want to* think *about her having sex.*

"I know I might be overstepping my boundaries, but I've known Alana for so many years. I really care about her, and since her mom's not around to make sure her reproductive health is cared for, I'd love to recommend a gynecologist for her. She really should've gone as soon as she started her menstrual cycle."

"Well, I don't want her to think that it's okay with me that she has sex. 'Cause it's not!"

"Would you rather she hide it and not be prepared and end up pregnant?"

"I need a drink," I replied.

"I'll write her a new prescription, and just give me a call sometime this week about the birth control issue, OK?"

"All right, thanks," I said. I stood to shake her hand. Wiped my moist hands on my jeans and headed out into the lobby.

Alana stood as I exited the office. I wrapped my arm around her shoulders and we left Dr. Weinstein's office.

We got back in the car and Alana immediately put her earplugs on and began listening to her iPod again. It had been a long time since her temper flared so wildly; I felt like I didn't know my own child. I was buggin' out by the evil twin she'd just introduced Dr. Weinstein and myself to. But I took the doctor's advice and didn't mention a thing about what had just went down.

I knew one thing: *It is time to meet this Parker clown.*

Chapter 8

Cassie

"What you need to do is get checked out, since Brice has been double-dippin' his spoon, if ya know what I mean," Tasha told me.

I'd already made the appointment, though. There was only one time, about a month ago, that we made love unprotected, and that was only because we'd both had one drink too many. But I made the appointment anyway, because I knew all too well that it only takes once.

"Girl, you already know," I said, cradling my cordless phone between my head and shoulders as I cornrowed Mia's hair. "So where're we going tonight?"

"Oh, yeah, let's hit up Vanilla Sky in the Village. It's 'models and bottles' night."

"And wherever there's models, there'll be plenty of men."

"Exactly," Tasha agreed.

"OK, so I'll be at your house around ten."

"Cool, 'cause I should be back with the babysitter by then."

I hung up the phone and threw it down on the bed next to me.

I had Mia call Brice when we'd first gotten home. There was no answer, so it looked like Mia would be going over to Tasha's after all.

Mia sniffled. I could tell she was crying. Her little body shaking, just a little.

"You are so tender-headed," I complained. "Just be still now so I can finish this head."

She didn't respond right away. Just kept weeping softly.

The alarm went off in my head, but I tried to maintain my composure. *I don't think I'll ever get used to this.*

"OK, baby. Are you hurting again?" I inhaled. Trapped the air inside my lungs. Closed my eyes. Steadied myself for the worst. My fingertips immediately becoming cold and numb.

"Mommy," she began, "it's OK. It's not that. You're just pulling my hair too tight, Mommy. Can we take a break?" she whined.

I exhaled, letting the warm air slowly escape from my lungs.

"Sure, honey. Just five minutes, though, OK?"

"OK," she cheerily replied as she sprang up from the floor and gave me a hug.

What happened to the tears?

"Can I have a fruit snack, please?"

"Go 'head," I agreed, shooing her off with a wave of my hand.

I silently cursed myself for being so easily alarmed.

So easily riled up. But Mia is my baby girl. She's all I got!

Although she'd only had two or three bad episodes, sickle-cell anemia was nothing to take lightly. The last time she said her legs and arms felt like bees were stinging her from the inside. She screamed and wriggled around and cried and kicked. It lasted for hours. I was too through, trying to soothe her and keep my own self composed. Then there were other times when she just got really tired and felt weak. Those days I let her miss school and I stayed home from work to take care of her.

Brice and I both carry the sickle-cell trait the doctors told us. Which meant that there was a one-in-four chance that one of our kids would be born with it. Well, since Mia's the only child we had, I guess we'd be OK if we had three more together.

Mia returned from the kitchen with her snack and plopped back down in between my legs, oblivious to the conflict going on inside my head.

"OK. Time's up! I'm ready, and I promise I won't cry anymore," she pledged.

We settled back in. I grabbed my comb and jumped back into braiding her hair; we were almost done.

Mia was intently watching "Maya + Miguel" on PBS, so I tuned out and my mind wandered back to the moment when the doctor delivered the news of Mia's health to us.

* * *

She was just a few hours old when the doctor told us of her diagnosis. Well, hell, how did they even know to test her? I asked. He then told us that more than forty states now require the test be done at birth.

"OK, so what are you telling us? Are you telling me there's something wrong with my baby?" I said, restating the obvious. But, shit, I was emotional after just delivering her.

"How is this going to affect her? What do we need to do, Doc?" Brice inquired.

"The short and easy answer is that her blood cells are shaped like crescents and should be round and flat so they can easily flow through blood vessels and carry oxygen throughout the body. Since some of her red blood cells have this crescent shape, they clog the blood vessels and die.

"She may be more tired than other children her age, use the bathroom more frequently, and her growth progress won't be the same as her peers. She'll have trouble fighting infections too. The most difficult part for her, and you as parents, may be comforting her through a pain crisis. She will experience pain, sometimes very severe, in the chest, legs, arms, shoulders and/or hips. This pain can last a few moments or a few days. It's hard to tell, because each case I see of sickle-cell anemia is so different."

"Is there a cure? Will she be on medicine to help suppress these attacks?" Brice asked. I was unable to move, let alone ask any more questions. My mind raced like I was on speed. I couldn't grasp most of what the doctor was saying and was annoyed that Brice was accepting this bullshit.

"No, there's no cure. But some children with this disease take a daily dose of penicillin to help ward off infections, and some also take a supplement of folic acid as well."

The doctor was mistaken, I was sure. Misdiagnosis happened all the time. *I'll sue this fucking hospital as soon as I prove they'd misdiagnosed my baby girl,* I thought.

"Where is she?" I yelled with contempt. The doctor was still talking. Carrying on about us being strong and that advances are being made every day with this disease. He was passing Brice a couple brochures about sickle-cell anemia when I yelled again. "Bring me my daughter. I need to see her now!"

"Sure. I'll have the nurse bring her in. I'm really sorry about your daughter, but she'll be a happy little girl. She has two loving parents, and I'm sure you'll get her the best care possible."

That night I refused the nurse's offer to take Mia into the nursery. Brice slept on the cot next to us. She slept in my arms and I didn't catch a wink from staring into her beautiful face all night.

Chapter 9

Payton

"I'm leaving," I yelled up to Alana from the foyer.

"I'm about to be out too," she yelled back.

"Where're you going?" I wondered. She hadn't told me she'd be going anywhere that night.

Alana came hopping down the stairs, looking way too casual for a Saturday night out.

"No, where are *you* going?" She stopped suddenly at the bottom of the stairs. Looking me up and down, she said, "Damn, Daddy, you're really trying to impress, huh?"

"What you talking about?" I asked nervously. "Get outta here."

"No, Daddy, you look really nice. I guess you're trying to look for Summer's replacement tonight."

"So you heard us last night?"

"Did I? She was screaming her ass off. What a bitch."

"Watch your mouth."

"Well, I'm just glad she's gone. She's a bird, Daddy. You deserve a classy chick, ya know?"

"Yeah, yeah. So where're you going tonight? You don't look like *you're* trying to impress anyone."

"Oh, I'm babysitting for Tasha again tonight."

"Tasha?"

"Yes, Daddy, remember that woman that responded to my ad I posted at the grocery store and dry cleaners?"

"Oh, yeah."

"She should be here any minute to pick me up."

"Well, I'll wait 'cause I want to meet her."

"She's cool, Daddy. Just go."

"No, I'll wait."

"All right," she agreed, walking away from me defiantly.

I followed her into the kitchen, where she began packing her book bag with snacks. One might wonder why would I have my daughter watch and be responsible for someone's child after what I walked in on in her therapy session today. When we got back in the car, she apologized and cried profusely. I told her that we will work to forget about this if she took one of her pills right then. Her behavior becomes a little less irrational when she's had one. She tried to protest but I reminded her about her babysitting job this weekend and that I would not allow it to happen unless she took her medication. Reluctantly she agreed and I watched her swallow the small, orange pill with some water.

I broke from my zoning when I heard Alana.

"When're you gonna buy me a car anyway?" she asked, placing her hands on her hips, expectantly.

"Here you go," I replied, sighing.

The doorbell rang and saved us from yet another conversation about me buying her a car. Alana went to answer it.

I was planning to surprise her for graduation, but if she kept harassing me, she wasn't going to get anything. What is the rush in getting a car, anyway? All of her girlfriends have cars and they are all eager to drive Alana wherever she needs to go.

"Daddy, this is Tasha."

Gotdamn! my mind yelled. Tasha was off the hook. My eyes remained cool as I took a quick survey of her body.

Thick, not chubby. A little bit of a pouch in her stomach, but most women my age have that because they've already had kids. I don't mind it, though. Statuesque in stature. Large, expressive eyes. Light brown. Maybe hazel. Contacts? Maybe not. Her skin was glistening, almost like she'd just stepped out of the shower. Her scent invaded the kitchen. A strong Egyptian musk. Her outfit—tight and short—leaving her womanly assets out for display. But not too much. Just enough. I felt my dick jump and stiffen just a bit. But then I remembered Summer and how I felt the same way I first saw her, and my dick went limp quick. Real quick.

"Tasha, this is my daddy, Payton," Alana continued her introductions.

I stood to shake her hand.

"I don't usually dress like this," Tasha said, looking a little embarrassed. "But I'm hitting the club tonight. I don't get out that often."

"Yeah, me too. My boy's dragging me out."

"Oh, really?" she said, smiling. *Beautiful smile. Down boy!* "Where're you going?"

"Negril, on West Third in the city."

"Oh, okay. I've been there a few times. The dance floor is small, though. We're headed to Vanilla Sky."

"I've heard good things about that place," I told her.

"OK, OK," Alana interjected. "I get paid by the hour and I need to get on the clock. Break it up."

"Shut up, Alana." I laughed. Tasha looked nervously at the kitchen floor.

We turned to leave the kitchen. I switched off the lights, and me and the girls headed toward the door.

Ugh, I thought. *Why is Tasha wearing such a long-ass weave, though?* At least it was a decent one. Like she visited the salon regularly. Her heels clicked down my hallway. Shiny, expensive-looking black shoes with a high, pointy heel. Pumps. Maybe stilettos. I didn't know, but her feet were arched enough to accentuate the muscles in her calves, which made her ass sit high and proud.

Damn, women are the devil.

"I'll have her back first thing in the morning, OK?" Tasha said, smiling brightly.

Is she flirting with me? Leave me alone, devil.

"OK, but not too early. Take your time."

Am I flirting back? Stop it, dumbass!

"Bye-bye, Daddy. Have fun, OK?" Alana said, giving me a hug and kiss on the cheek.

"All right, sweetie, see you tomorrow."

"Be safe and don't be looking for no replacements tonight."

"Here you go. Good night, Alana." I sighed, playfully pushing her away from me. "It was nice meeting you, Tasha. Don't hurt nobody, girl."

She cracked up. "Nice meeting you too."

I hopped in my car and called Damon.

"Yo, I'm on my way. You ready?"

We arrived at Negril in a little over an hour. Damon had to stop off and get his car washed at one of those twenty-four-hour car washes in the city first.

Our boy Eric was at the door, so we got in free. Gave a pound in greeting to the DJ. We knew him too. And yup, Niecy was at the bar, so we knew we'd get strong drinks all night.

"We gotta find another spot," I told Damon. "We know almost every person in here."

"You're right about that one, playa."

"Hey, Niecy," I sang, approaching the bar. It wasn't too crowded yet. Niecy was looking delicious as always. She had on a black bustier that made her breasts damn near touch her chin. Her face was heavily made up with pink-and-lime-green makeup. Her lime-green-and-pink-striped skirt was short . . . and let's just say, if Niecy wanted to, she could serve drinks on her ass. But as always she was all up on Damon's tip. I was the nice guy that got overlooked most of the time. Damon was the cocky dickhead that women threw themselves at.

"Hey, boys. The usual?" she yelled over the music, winking and swinging her long, curly hair off her shoulders.

"You know it," Damon replied.

Niecy poured us each a shot of Hennessy and a Heineken.

"To gettin' bitches," Damon yelled, hoisting his shot glass in the air.

I just shook my head, a silent protest to his crudeness, and met his glass in the air.

We sucked down the liquid love and guzzled half a bottle of beer to chase it down.

That was our appetizer course. We were just getting warmed up. Niecy was mixing up our main courses already.

"Two Incredible Hulks for my two favorite men," Niecy said with her sexy Caribbean accent.

"Thanks, baby," Damon said, handing her sixty dollars. "We're good for a while."

We took our green drinks and headed toward the front of the club to have a seat. The DJ was rocking "Poison" by BBD and the crowd was getting a little hype. There are a couple of songs that no matter how old they are, they could still get a crowd excited. "Poison" was one of them. A couple people were getting up and dancing.

Mostly couples that night. Dance floor wasn't big enough for real dancing.

"So, is it really over with you and Summer? I thought she was the one, homie," Damon teased.

"Yeah, but don't we always think that in the beginning? Shit is always sweet in the beginning."

"What happened, though? Just last week y'all was OK."

"She's crazy, man. Well, you know she's always beefing with Alana and shit. And she's always nagging and nagging. She's not keeping herself up. I just got tired of her shit. And she was never the *one*. She was just a placeholder."

"How was that gushy stuff?"

"Damn, man. You have tunnel vision. I don't kiss and tell."

"I didn't ask how she kisses."

"Honestly, she wasn't even all that in the bed either. You know if it was blazing, I would've at least wanted to stay friends."

"Exactly. Platonic pussy. I feel you."

"Platonic pussy, huh?"

All we could do was laugh at his ignorant self. The club was filling up slowly. Seemed like more couples than anything. Some people were just downstairs having a few drinks before heading upstairs to the restaurant to eat. There were two groups of women there that weren't coupled up. But they looked young. The twenty-one-to-twenty-five crowd was off-limits for me. I was done with young girls. Way too much drama.

Damon was looking bored. I was feeling a little buzzed. We needed a little something more.

"Hey, man, I heard Vanilla Sky was poppin' tonight," I told him.

I wondered if I really just wanted to see Tasha again. *Na,* I decided. I just wanted to go somewhere where there was more people and a bigger dance floor. *Yeah, that was it.*

"Oh, yeah, I heard of that place. Wanna head over there? We're gonna have to take a cab, 'cause I paid a grip for all-night parking, and I'm not moving my car just to go somewhere else and have to pay again."

"Quit ya bitchin', man. This cute shorty I know is gonna be there too."

"Oh, let me find out that's why you really wanna go. Looking for a little something, huh?" Damon probed.

"Na, son. I said she's cute. Real cute. But not really my type. I know you'd like her, though."

I knew I had him hooked. Damon went back and whispered his good-byes in Niecy's ear and kissed her on the cheek. She blushed like it was the first time she'd ever been kissed. I waved to her from across the room.

I finally admitted to myself that Tasha was heavy on my mind, but Alana was her babysitter. If she and I didn't work out, then Alana would be out of a job. Things would be awkward. It just wasn't the ideal situation. Plus, I was being truthful to Damon. She was definitely more his type.

Chapter 10

Cassie

I saw him when he first walked in. He looked as fine as he wanted to be. Our eyes met momentarily; then we both looked away bashfully.

Tasha and I were tipsy already. Vanilla Sky wasn't as packed as it usually was. We'd gotten a booth that was usually designated for VIPs, but since it was kinda dead that night, Tasha and I got the VIP treatment.

My eyes followed him and his friend to the bar.

"Look, Tash," I said, pointing his way.

I didn't go for the video-ho look that night. Tasha held that title down. I was casual chic—couldn't muster up the gumption to put together a vixen look. I was wearing black skinny jeans, the gold Jimmy Choos that Brice had bought me a couple years ago and a cream tube top with gold embroidery. Had on my gold bamboo earrings and my old-school nameplate around my neck. I combed some Curly Pudding (the little bit I still had left) into my hair and let it hang wild and free, resting just above my earlobes.

"What is he doing here?" Tasha yelled over Jay-Z's voice pumping out of the speakers.

"How'd he know I was even here?" I wondered.

"You really think he somehow found out you were coming here tonight and followed you here? Don't flatter yourself, honey," Tasha said, waving her hand.

"Absolutely."

"Yeah, you might be right about that, girl," she admitted. "You have got some kinda hold on him. What you got between your legs, platinum?"

The alcohol running through my veins made me laugh at Tasha's joke, but this shit wasn't funny. How was I supposed to enjoy myself with Brice at the same club?

He started straight toward our booth.

"Here we go. This is going to be a long night," I told Tasha.

He nodded, saying, "Hi, ladies." Then kept it moving toward the men's room in the rear of the club.

"Hey, Brice, what's up?" Tasha offered, but he was already long gone.

"What the hell was that? I don't like the way!" I was taken aback by his nonchalance.

"Ha! And you thought he was here to stalk your ass. He ain't even thinking 'bout you. I take back your platinum status," Tasha joked.

It stung. Not sure why it did, but it did.

"It's OK. You got that one, Tash."

"He just walked by you like you was nothing, girl." She laughed even harder.

"I don't even care. Shoot, order us another round. I'm here to have fun. Fuck Brice."

"More like, you want to fuck Brice."

"All right, you're corny now. Quit while you're ahead."

Tasha was cracking herself up. It was all good, though. The decision to end my relationship with Brice was mine.

Brice emerged from the bathroom and walked through the small crowd on the other side of the room.

Tasha had motioned for the waitress to bring us another round.

Then two brothas walked up in front of our booth, blocking my view.

"Hey, Payton!" Tasha screamed as she jumped up from behind the table and hugged him. "This is my best friend, Cassie. Cassie, this is my babysitter's father, Payton."

"Oh, OK. Nice to meet you," I said, standing to extend my hand.

"Cassie, Tasha, this is my boy Damon," Payton announced.

We stood there, not knowing what to do next. The decent thing to do would be to invite them to sit, but I really didn't feel like being up under no men that night.

Payton was sexy, cute, innocent-looking. Damon was on fire, though! But he wasn't thinking about me; his eyes were tearing through Tasha's clothes.

Tasha was blushing. Payton started laughing. So did I. Damon caught himself. Looked embarrassed.

Payton said, "If you're going to eye fuck her all night, you could at least buy her a drink."

Tasha stopped blushing long enough to giggle at Payton's joke. Damon tried to play to cool, but it was far too late for that.

"Hey, man, we are standing with the finest two ladies in this whole place. Show some respect, dog."

"So, can we buy you some drinks?" Payton asked.

"Actually, we just ordered another round, but you can get the next one," I said politely.

Tasha was being all quiet, trying to play cool. That's how I knew she was feeling Mr. Damon.

Since Tasha was stuck on stupid, and I was tired of standing up, I offered the guys a seat at our booth.

They took a seat and sandwiched Tasha and me in the middle just as the waitress delivered our drinks. The guys ordered Heinekens, and Tasha suggested we all take a lemon drop shot.

Out of the corner of my eye, I saw Brice watching. Eyes dripping with jealousy.

"So, Cassie," Payton began, turning toward me, "how do you know Tasha?"

We were the leftovers—forced to communicate by process of elimination. Damon and Tasha had that immediate attraction, which left us two to tend to one another.

Payton was definitely my type—well, physically anyway. Who knew what he had going on mentally and otherwise? But after the incident with Brice the night before, I had to push the attraction I felt away. I refused to jump from the frying pan into the fire. From my baby's daddy to someone else's damn baby-daddy.

"Oh, Tasha and I go way back," I said, not really feeling like getting into it.

"Cool, cool," he said nodding. There was a mean silence between us. I sensed a strong mutual attraction going on, but I had too much baggage. I had enough baggage to take a trip to Italy for a month. And who knew how much he was carrying?

I looked around the club, avoiding eye contact with the fine man beside me.

Damon had his arm around Tasha. They were giggling like idiots.

"So what do you do, Payton?" I inquired, trying to make small talk and not be rude.

"I'm a gym teacher and basketball coach for Dolan Middle School. Basically, an overpaid babysitter for overaged babies. But since school is out on summer vacation, I'm the director over at Horizons Day Camp."

I was getting antsy; the liquor was making my vision blurry, fingertips tingly.

"But you look bored with my life," he noticed. "You wanna dance? Give the lovebirds some privacy?" he joked, nodding toward Damon and Tasha.

It wasn't really a question because he had already stood up and taken my hand.

"Sure," I agreed, happy to release some energy.

I followed Payton to the dance floor, the DJ was playing "Dutty Wine." A few chicks were leaning forward, swinging their heads around in circles, knees moving in and out like they were doing the Funky Chicken. Looked like they were going to break their necks. I knew if I tried, I would surely break mine.

Payton swayed from side to side, doing a conservative two-step. Definitely had rhythm, but I could tell reggae wasn't his forte.

I stood in front of him, winding my waist like a pro. He pulled me in closer. The song changed to "Girls Dem Sugar," with Beenie Man and Mya.

I began winding a little deeper, slowly thrusting my pelvis toward him. I stepped away a little, embarrassed about my forward gesture.

He grabbed me by the waist and turned me around so that I could back it up on him. So I did.

Just as I felt him stiffen under his pants, I felt a sharp pain shoot through my right shoulder.

"Ouch!" I screamed as extreme dizziness hit me. I spun around quickly to see what caused the pain.

Brice was planted in front of me with his nose flaring like a bull's. He'd grabbed me by the arm to get me away from Payton, like I was his damn piece of property.

"Get your hands off me," I screamed, jerking my arm from his grip.

"Who the fuck is this, Cassie? So this is who you're fucking?" Brice fired, grabbing my arm again.

"Yo, playboy, you need to let the lady go," Payton ordered Brice.

"It's OK, Payton. You don't need to get involved," I said, rubbing my arm. Suddenly I was completely sober.

"Tell your man something before he gets hurt," Brice told me, referring to Payton.

Payton stepped up in Brice's face, daring him to do something.

Damon and Tasha came flying over, out of nowhere.

"We got a problem here, P?" Damon asked, glaring straight at Brice. Seeming to address him and not Payton at all.

My heart was torn. Brice had never put his hands on me before. I hated him so much right then, but I didn't want to see him get hurt either. Damon was just waiting on Payton to give him the word so he could let loose.

"Do we?" Payton asked Brice, offering him a chance to back down.

Brice backed down.

"My bad. Na, we're cool. No problem here," he said, backing away from Payton. He didn't walk away, though. Just stood there a couple feet away from Payton, looking for my eyes to reveal how I was feeling.

Damon looked cocky. *They'd won the battle.*

Payton's eyes met mine. They were filled with concern.

Tasha just looked at the ground. It was awkward. Tasha and I went way back with Brice, and these new dudes, we'd just met, were avenging my honor like we'd known each other for years. Punking someone we both revered as family even through all the turmoil of our sordid relationship.

Security was quickly approaching. The standoff was causing too much attention.

"C'mon, guys. Let's just go back to our booth," I suggested.

"So you just gonna go over there with him, like I don't even exist?" Brice asked.

"Brice, we'll talk later. Right now I'm out with my friends having a good time. That was until you came and ruined it."

Security had reached us.

"Is there a problem here?" the bald guard asked.

"Na," Brice answered. "Not anymore. I'm about to solve it."

Everything that happened next happened so quickly, I don't even remember how my shirt got ripped and how I lost an earring. But the next thing I knew, Brice punched Payton in the face. Payton was stunned, but it was only a hot second before he returned the punch. He missed, though, because security had yoked Brice up and was already dragging him toward the door. The second security guard had Payton pinned up too. Damon tried rushing past the security to get at Brice but failed. Those security guards were solid as hell.

Tasha and I stood there dumbfounded by what just happened and unsure where our allegiance should lie.

"Should we go make sure they're OK?" I asked.

"Hell no. Look at you. Shirt ripped, and where's your earring? If they want to behave like cavemen, that's on them. Let's go get right, 'cause you're looking a damn mess."

New Yorkers are a trip. So jaded. I was sure that everyone would've stopped and been staring, considering all that had just transpired. But, nope, I glanced around as we headed toward the bathroom and everyone was minding their own business and having a good time.

Tasha was right—I was a bubbling hot mess. I finger-combed my hair back into its proper coif, while Tasha used the bathroom. We both stood at the sinks washing our hands.

"Girl, can you believe it?" she squealed.

"Don't even go there. Let's pretend this did not just happen."

"I don't like the way!" She belted out our favorite line, laughing at the situation. See, "I don't like the way" can mean many things. It can be good as in "I don't like the way that brother is fine!" Or it can be negative as in "I don't like the way that bitch is looking at me." But since Tasha and I are so close, there's no need to even finish the

sentence. Just a simple "I don't like the way!" will do, and we'll know exactly what the other means.

She made me laugh too. "Yeah me neither," I agreed.

"Payton didn't even get close enough to *smell* the platinum pussy yet and he's fighting over you."

"Tasha, shut up, girl. Let's get outta here."

We left the club with smiles on our faces, refusing to reveal the embarrassment we felt on the inside about the scene that had just ended only moments before.

Chapter 11

Payton

Sometimes I don't mind the rain. Sometimes it's soothing, therapeutic. Not that day.

That day it was annoying. Incessant. Like sleet hitting a tin roof. Loud. Obnoxious.

I was half hungover from the night before. My right eye was almost swollen shut from that sucker punch that Brice delivered. *Punk ass.*

But I had more pressing issues that afternoon. My head was reeling. Mind racing from the letter I received yesterday.

No return address.

Postmarked from Brooklyn, New York.

I'm a pretty private person, so I didn't call Damon up when I got the letter. Didn't drag Alana away from her never-ending myspace.com perusal to tell her about the letter.

Just sat there. On the edge of my bed. Staring down at my hands. Rain pounding on my roof.

I almost wanted to cry.

Probably should've been crying.

But I was too pissed to shed a tear. Pissed. Confused. Betrayed. Incensed. Angered.

I was still holding on to the letter.

It was from my presumed-dead ex-wife.

The letter read:

> Payton,
> Where do I begin? First, let me say I'm sorry. Please don't be too upset. It took me years to get better and a couple more years to conjure up enough courage to write this letter.
> Obviously, I'm not dead or missing.
> Not physically, but for a while there, my mind was dead. The drugs had control of me. Well, let me back up. . . .
> I don't even think you knew I was strung out. Did you? You probably thought I was just cheating on you. Well, I guess I was doing that too, but that was all after the addiction started.
> OK, remember my cousin Ray? Remember he used to be like my best friend? I used to share with him about how boring my life had become since I had Alana and we got married. One night he introduced me to this guy, Larry. Larry introduced me to ice. You probably know ice as crystal meth. Larry would mix it up right in his kitchen. It made me feel so good. Helped me forget about the responsibilities I had weighing me down. I was free! Ice gave me the excitement I was lacking in my life.
> I loved you and I never intended to cheat on you, but the ice had me strung out there.

How's Sugar?

I miss my daughter so much! I only have one picture of her. The picture I had on my key chain the night I left. It wasn't my intention to leave you and Sugar that night. I just couldn't come back. I just couldn't. Something so bad happened that running away from everyone and everything was easier than facing what I'd done.

My family always had high hopes for me. I was the good girl. I was supposed to break the cycle. Knowing the mess that I'd gotten myself so caught up in, I knew that night that I was no better than my sorry-ass mother and sisters. That was the worse thing I've ever felt.

I didn't come back home that night. Couldn't. Moved to North Carolina with Larry. There I was Jane Doe. No expectations. No responsibilities. I was happy. I had Larry and an endless supply of ice.

Until Larry didn't come home one night. I had enough ice to get me through the week, so I didn't care. Then my supply was gone and Larry still hadn't resurfaced.

Rent was due. I didn't have any money, so I had to leave. Then there's a period of time right after that, that's still a blur to me. I'll just say that I did what I had to do to survive. I was on crystal meth and ecstasy for a while. Then I got hooked on heroin and that's when shit got ugly.

I'm all better now, though. Did a couple years in the pen. Clean now. Living in Brooklyn with my two kids (yes, I had two more kids!) and my fiancé.

Which brings me back around to why I'm writing this letter.

I want a divorce. Ha! Sounds funny, huh? But we're still legally married, aren't we?

You're probably not laughing right now, but it just sounds so strange.

Also, I want to see Sugar. I need to let her know my story. I want to be in her life.

Is she going to college? How beautiful did she turn out?

Now I'm crying. Going to end here. I owe you a big thank-you for taking care of my child. I know she's a gem because of you.

Payton, I can't erase the past, but I damn sure want to make things right for my future.

And my future begins with making things right with Sugar. Please call me at 718-555-2783. I wait patiently for your call.

Keisha

Chapter 12

Cassie

It was a lazy Sunday. Mia was still at Tasha's house and I just wanted to lay around feeling sorry for myself. It was raining outside, so that gave me further motivation to throw myself a pity party. The night before was a disaster. The night before that was a disaster. *Today is a better day*, I tried to convince my sorry ass.

I owed Payton an apology, though. I'd put him in a predicament the night before that would have been crazy for anyone—let alone someone that I'm not even involved with. He took up for me. Protected me like I was his lover. I wasn't used to that type of treatment from someone I wasn't sleeping with.

Tasha got Payton's number from Damon that morning and called to give it to me. I was torn. I didn't want to call him and seem thirsty. He was cute and just my type, but I just wasn't at a point in my life to open up to another man. I needed some time alone. From last night's display he seemed mature enough not to misconstrue my honest-to-goodness apology for me trying to get at him.

So I dialed. And he picked up.

Damn, I thought. It would've been perfect if he didn't pick up. I could've just left a voice mail and been done with it.

"Hello?" he asked again, sounding a bit agitated.

"Hi, Payton, this is Cassie. I met you last night at Vanilla Sky," I blurted out.

Why the hell did I have to say all that? Of course he knows who I am, dumbass. It was only the night before. Was I getting nervous? Cassie, apologize and get off the phone with this man.

"Yes, I know who you are, Cassie," he said mockingly, followed by a chuckle. His voice was deep, smooth and sexy.

"So, Payton, I just called to apologize for last night. I mean, I've never seen Brice get violent like that. I had no idea."

"Na, its OK, Cassie. I know you were just out trying to have a good time. It's OK."

"Yeah, but still. It shouldn't have happened. Please accept my apology, Payt."

"Payt? I can't say that anyone has ever called me that." He was busting with laughter.

"What's wrong with 'Payt'? You never heard of a nickname? You know, a shortened version of your gov'ment?" I teased.

"My family and some of my boys call me P. Just P. But you can call me Payt if you want. It's cool."

I giggled. Don't know why, but I did. Talking

to Payton lightened my mood, if only momentarily. Knowing he wasn't holding a grudge made me feel better. But being given the privilege of being able to call him "Payt" would require me to actually speak to him again after we hung up, and I had no intention of speaking to him again anytime soon.

"OK, Payt, I'll be able to sleep well tonight knowing that you forgive me," I blurted out, trying to end the conversation before it got too awkward. My efforts were in vain, because we ended up on the phone for hours.

My other line beeped in before he could answer with his good-byes. The number read private, but I answered anyway.

"Hello?"

"Who's this?" the female voice aggressively asked.

"Oh, OK, maybe you didn't realize that you were calling my damn house. *Who's this?*"

Now it had been a minute since I fielded one of these calls. And it never failed that it was one of Brice's jump-offs looking for trouble. Usually, we'd go at it, but since I was through with him, there wouldn't be an argument this time around. I remained collected, for the most part.

"Um, did you hear me?" I asked again, now matching the aggressive tone she had started the conversation with.

"Bitch," she yelled, and hung up.

Ugh. That call just made me resent Brice even

more because of the dumb, young shit that comes along with being involved with a man-whore.

I clicked back over.

"I'm sorry," I offered. "That was a prank call. I feel like I'm in high school again," I told Payton.

"A prank call? From who?"

"Judging from the fact that she just called me a bitch and hung up in my face, I'd say it was someone that Brice is dealing with."

"Wait a minute. Are you serious?" Payton asked with a hearty laugh. "No, I can believe it. I've dealt with my share of nonsense. Yup, that one sounds all too familiar actually."

"Oh, so I guess you've dealt with some unsavory people in your day too, huh?"

"Man, listen. I could tell you some stories."

"I got time," I said, realizing how desperate I sounded for company, and immediately feeling like a fool. I held my breath, hoping he'd say something to make me feel better.

He laughed. Now this was, like, the third time since we got on the phone that he got a laugh at my expense.

Or was he just as nervous as I was?

"I don't think you're even halfway ready to know the kind of nonsense I've been through. I don't want to risk scaring you away before I get to know you better," he said with an abrupt pause.

And again there was a sloppy pause. Like he realized he'd said something to put himself out there.

Just like I had done moments before. I let him sweat for a minute before I broke up the awkwardness. Like he did with me, I laughed. *Touché.*

I couldn't even remember the last time I'd had a conversation with a man, other than Brice, over the phone. And when Brice and I did talk on the phone, it was to schedule a booty call. It felt good. My mood was elevating with every minute I spent on the phone with him. I didn't want to hang up. And if I wasn't mistaken, he sounded like he was in a bit of a funk when I first called, and now he seemed to be enjoying this silly conversation too.

"So let's skip the insanity that is our love lives. Where'd you grow up?" I asked him.

"Right here. Stamford born and raised. How 'bout you?"

"Me too. Lived on Custer Street most of my life, but when I was twelve, we moved to the Cove."

"Oh, excuse me, y'all moved on up, huh? I lived in Greenwich Village, way back when it was actually still 'the Village,' until I graduated high school."

"Oh, please, no, times were still hard. Wait a minute. There's no way you went to Stamford High, I would've known you."

"Yeah, I got kicked out of Stamford High, early freshman year, so I ended up going to West Hill. And you don't know nothing about hard times until you lived in the Village."

"Kicked out for what? And yes, I do know about hard times. Custer Street was no Mayberry."

"All right, Cassie, if you say so. I got kicked out for pulling a knife out on this senior cat trying to act tough and shit 'cause I was a freshman."

"That was you!" I squealed. "You're a legend at Stamford High. That is too funny. Wait till I tell Tasha who you are! And yes, I do say so, we were poor!"

We'd all heard about the freshman that almost sliced up Kevin, the wannabe thug of the senior class. Ever since he got punked that day, he lost all his juice. Well, that's what we called it back then—juice.

"We were so poor that I had to wear my big sister's hand-me-downs," he joked.

"We were so poor that my father made us wear our coats to bed in the winter because he refused to turn on the heat?"

"Least your father was around. We were so poor that we had to put water in our cereal sometimes."

"You ever had to eat a mayonnaise sandwich?"

"What you know about sugar water?"

"How 'bout we were so poor we had to use the oven for heat?"

"How 'bout we were so poor, me, my mother and two sisters had to use the fire escape to leave the building every morning to avoid seeing the landlord?"

"OK, now that's not poor, that's just sad. You won," I admitted in defeat.

We shared another laugh and the conversation graduated to more adult things, like college. I only took those classes that Brice forced me to.

Payton had graduated from UConn, and once his daughter went away, he was planning to start classes to get his master's degree. He had goals; he didn't want to be a gym teacher forever.

Then the conversations shifted to our kids. I didn't tell him anything about Mia's sickle-cell anemia. Not that I was embarrassed, but it was just a very private, emotional issue. Not to be shared with someone I barely knew. He gloated like any proud father would over his daughter, Alana. And also mentioned how she had a past of not liking his girlfriends. We both blurted out that we were staying clear of any relationships right now. Agreeing that the biggest mistake after a recent breakup was to get immediately involved with someone else.

It was early into the evening when Payton and I finally got off the phone. I had to go pick up Mia from Tasha's house, so I got ready and headed out.

Talking to Payt was nice. Innocent. Like it used to feel back in high school when you met someone new. He didn't ask to see me again. I was relieved, but at the same time disappointed. While I wanted to see him again, just as friends, I knew that we'd be risking the chance of crossing that line, because there was a shared attraction and the instant chemistry we had over the phone was crazy.

Chapter 13

Payton

It was good talking to Cassie last night. I'd never had such an enjoyable conversation with Summer, which further made me realize I'd made the right choice dumping her. I hadn't heard from her since I listened to her dozen messages in Dr. Weinstein's waiting room the day before. But I knew this was just the calm before the storm. Women like her didn't like to lose, and everything needed to be on their terms. Her ego was going to make her lose her mind, I was sure of it. Unbeknownst to her, she'd be about to start losing her mind on someone who was not in the right frame of mind—me.

My mind was all messed up after remembering that letter from Keisha's sorry ass. First I folded the letter up and hid it under my mattress, not sure whether to show Alana or not. I took a nap, but I was haunted by thoughts of Keisha. And *that* night. The last time I'd seen her. *That* call. So eerie. The urgency in her voice. I'd had nightmares about that night for a very long time, and just over the past few years, I had been able to stop dreaming and thinking about it. The dreams were back that afternoon as I lay in bed, bothered by the hissing rain.

Back then, after she first disappeared, I'd dream about her every night. Sometimes I dreamt she was raped and kidnapped and thrown in the ocean. I pictured her face splattered with blood, frozen in fear, eyes wide open, knees shaking. Nervous. Scared. Other times the dreams weren't so bad; she left us and moved to Africa to be a missionary. Or once she just simply died. Quietly in her sleep. There was no fear, no pain. She just peacefully passed on.

About a year after her disappearance the case went cold. I'd presumed she was dead. I mean, for what reason would a woman with a decent husband and a beautiful daughter at home run off? I can't even count the number of times I asked myself that. In my mind believing she was dead was an easier pill to swallow.

So I slept about an hour after reading the letter. Alana woke me to tell me she was going to the mall to meet Parker. I was groggy, but the mention of his name snapped me to my senses.

"You tell Parker I want to meet him, OK? And soon."

"Daddy," she whined.

"Daddy, nothing. If you want to keep seeing this kid, he needs to come by here so I can meet him."

"All right, all right," she surrendered. "I'll let

you know right before I leave. I gotta get dressed," she told me. "What happened to your eye? It looks swollen."

"Oh, this," I said, touching my eye. "I got elbowed in the club last night. This cat was dancing too wild."

"Hmmm. If you say so," she answered, walking away. Her tone let me know she saw right through my bullshit.

I sat up, still choking over the words I read in Keisha's letter, when the phone rang. I jumped at it, eager to have a distraction from my thoughts. It was Cassie calling to apologize from the night before. I thought it was a nice gesture, but I didn't have any hard feelings anyway. Plus, Brice hit like a bitch anyway.

We'd been on the phone for about twenty minutes when Alana crept back into my room.

"Who you on the phone with?" she rudely interrupted.

"None of your business," I told her.

"You all giddy and stuff. Must be a girl, huh?" she teased.

"Shut up. What you need, some money?"

"Yes, I do. But, Daddy, who you on the phone wit?" she insisted.

"My friend Cassie, nosey."

Alana grabbed my wallet off my dresser and passed it to me. I gave her a few bucks and shooed her out of my room.

Cassie and I ended up talking for hours, and

when we hung up, I was in a much better mood.
The rain had even stopped.

"Hey, Alana, come in here for a minute," I
called down the stairs. She'd just returned from
the mall a few minutes before.

Later on that evening I was in my bedroom,
at my desk, trying to figure out how to download
some songs to my iPod. Alana had bought me
the damn thing for my birthday, and three
months later I still hadn't had one song on it.
Guess not having a nagging, time-stealing girlfriend sucking the life out of me was giving me
time to catch up on some things I'd been meaning to get to.

"Yeah, Dad," she said, now behind me.

"Show me how to get some songs on here."

"First you have to download some songs and
save them in your library. Hook the iPod up to
the back of the computer. Then you can just
grab the songs from the library and drag and
drop 'em into the iPod icon."

She plugged the cord in and went to a Web
site to download some software.

"This is where you can go to search for almost
any song you can think of."

"OK. So show me how," I said, hovering over
her shoulder, impressed by her technical know-
how. Let her tell it, all of her friends can whiz
around the computer just like she does, and it
ain't no big deal. I'm just old school, she teases.

"Remember this one, Daddy?"

"Just the Two of Us" came blasting from my computer. It was *our* song. I reached my hand out, properly inviting her to dance with me. She accepted by grabbing my hand and walking toward me.

Alana laid her head on my chest and we rocked back and forth in the middle of my bedroom. Moments like this were priceless. When she wasn't arguing with or talking shit about one of my girl-friends. When she wasn't begging for money. When she wasn't complaining about her trifling friends. When she wasn't romanticizing over that punk, Parker. When she was just being my little girl.

We didn't speak the whole time. The silence made me reflect on how fast she'd grown up. Too fast. In a few weeks she'd be gone off to college already. Damn! I was sad to see her leave, but happy to see her go! Although I would take nine bullets for her, I have my needs, and she was putting a damper on my love life.

We slowly rocked back and forth. I was a proud father. Outside of a couple fights in school and having been suspended from school a couple times for mouthing off to her teachers, Alana is a good kid. Got great grades and was headed to college—New York University, at that. NYU offered her a full scholarship and all I had to pay for was room and board. I was relieved that she'd be far enough from home to stay out my business, but close enough to visit home whenever she wanted.

I've done a damn good job, I thought, allowing myself to be proud of my damn self for a moment. And I didn't have to pull out my shotgun and shoot at no little baggy-jean-wearing wannabe thugs for breaking her heart. *Damn, I did do well.* Smiling to myself, I soaked up the moment. Just about made it to the finish line. Keisha would be proud.

I'd allowed Keisha to trespass on my thoughts all day since receiving that letter. Still hadn't mentioned anything to Alana about it. Really, I needed to speak to Dr. Weinstein first to see if it'd be cool to let them see each other. I wasn't sure if it would be therapeutic for Alana. Maybe she'd be ecstatic to get to know her mother. But then again maybe she'd regress. Hate her mother. Lash out against her. I didn't want to make the decision on my own; I needed a professional opinion.

My personal opinion, though, was that although Keisha probably didn't deserve to see Alana's face again, she was her mother and had the right. I'd had long enough to search deep regarding my feelings for, rather against, Keisha, and I decided I was over it. Nothing was left in my heart for her. Not even contempt. It was so long ago, and Alana and I turned out okay without her ass.

The song ended and Alana sprang out of my arms, back into the seat in front of the computer.

"So, anyways, Daddy, you understand how to download the songs, right?"

"Yeah, I guess," I answered, knowing damn well I'd forgotten everything she'd just shown me before our dance. I'd figure it out, though.

"Oh, Daddy, I have a great idea!" she yelled, jumping up from the chair. Her energy was wearing *me* out.

"Yes, Sugar?"

"'Sugar'?" she asked, looking at me like I had an extra eye in the middle of my forehead.

"You don't remember I used to call you that when you were little?" I knew she didn't, and I silently damned Keisha for bringing that memory back to me. I hadn't called her "Sugar" since Keisha disappeared.

"No, I don't. It's cute, though. Anyways, Daddy, I have a great idea," she said, rubbing her hands together like she had just hatched the perfect plan.

I was still standing in the middle of the floor where we'd just shared our dance. Why? I don't know. Guess my mind was just overflowing with thoughts. I walked over closer to her.

"What's your big idea?"

"You know how you been having trouble finding a decent woman?"

She didn't wait for an answer before she went on. "Well, you should try putting a profile up on SexyCTSingles.com."

I stopped her mididea. Wasn't interested.

"No thanks, Alana, but I do all right meeting

women in person. I'm not desperate. I don't think I have to resort to those measures just yet."

"You're showing your age, Dad," she joked. "Look, it does not mean you're desperate because you try online dating. It has its benefits. First you get to see the person's picture and rule out all the women you aren't physically attracted to. Then you can initiate contact with the ones you find attractive and get to know their personalities."

"Uh-huh," I sighed, pretending to be listening. There was no way I was going to try this shit.

"OK, so then you can begin to eliminate those whose personality is not a fit with yours. Then you can begin to meet some in person and go from there."

"There are some psychos in this world, Alana."

"Summer was a damn psycho and you dealt with her for a good minute," she argued.

Good point, I thought.

"Anyways, you can see someone's religious beliefs, whether they have kids or not, if they've ever been married. If they smoke. What type of job they have. If they drink. I mean, you can learn so much about a person by reading their profile."

"Uh-huh," I sighed again.

"Now, you can't get all that information from meeting someone in a club, Daddy," she reasoned.

She double-clicked on the Internet icon

and within seconds was filling out a short questionnaire.

"Alana," I said, my tone informing her that she was pushing her luck.

"Daddy!" she said, challenging me. "OK, so your screen name could be"—she stopped typing to turn around to look at me.—"um, how 'bout ChocolateNCharming?"

"Get the hell outta here with that, girl. That sounds ridiculous."

I guess she took my disagreement with *that* particular name as me being open to hearing more and possibly agreeing to post a profile on this Web site. And I guess I could've shut down her idea, if I really wasn't feeling it. But she had a point—my love life was going nowhere.

"Um," she continued, looking me up and down. "Coach Blue? You're a coach and your favorite color is blue."

"No, Alana."

"Sugar. Call me Sugar, Daddy."

"So you like that nickname, baby?"

"That's it! Sugar's Daddy. That can be your screen name! And yes, I do like that name. Makes me feel like a little girl all over again." She smiled. Alana was in her element—poking around on the Internet and being the center of my attention.

Alana added all my preferences and harassed me to upload my picture. "Daddy, no one's going to want to talk to you without seeing your picture. It's just the way it is."

So I gave in again and we posted a picture of Damon and me going to his frat brother's wedding, with the caption clarifying that I was the one on the right.

That night I became Sugar's Daddy on Sexy-CTSingles.com.

Chapter 14

Cassie

When I arrived at Tasha's house to pick up Mia, Tasha was making dinner, in the kitchen and the girls were watching TV in Freesia's room.

"Mommy," Mia yelled when she heard my voice from the living room. Then she came running out and gave me a tight hug around my waist.

"Hey, momma-momma," I replied, stroking her hair.

Before I knew it, Freesia was screaming that the show was back on and Mia was sprinting back toward her bedroom.

"Hi, Auntie Cassie!" Freesia yelled from her room down the hall.

"Hi, baby!"

"So how you feeling today?" Tasha asked as I took a seat at her kitchen's island, which flanked the living room.

"I mean, a little better. It is what it is," I offered. "Called Payton to apologize about last night. He was really cool about the whole thing."

"Did Brice call you?" she wondered. "Girls, dinner's ready," she screamed toward the rear of her apartment.

"No, he didn't call me. I have no words for his ass anyway. Can you even believe him? Acting all jealous and shit like that?"

"I know you're not talking. When you yoked that girl up that time at Playland over him? Uh-huh, you don't want me to pull your card on that one."

"OK, that situation was different. He was my man then. We don't have anything now."

"Yeah, OK, whatever helps you sleep at night, babe," she retorted. "Girls, I said dinner's ready. Get in here."

The girls came bolting out of the room, realizing Tasha's tone was more serious this time.

"Now take your plates and go back in the room. Me and Auntie Cassie are having grown-up talk."

"OK, Mommy," Freesia agreed. The girls headed back to the room.

"Why did I end up talking to Payton for a couple hours?"

"What? Let me find out?" she teased.

"No, nothing like that, Tash. It was just . . . just talking. Felt good. He wasn't trying to holla. We were just kicking it, ya know?"

"Well, shit, you need to jump on that. Get Brice out of your mind. He's a trifling ass. He need to grow up."

"Yeah."

"And it's just about time you realize it. Stop wasting your time. His sorry-ass career ain't going nowhere. He's whack at going downtown anyway, right?"

I didn't recall sharing all that with her, but as many bashing sessions we had on Brice's expense, maybe I did.

"Well, damn. I mean, in the beginning he was whack, but I taught him the right way and it got a lot better over the years. But anyways, what does that have to do with anything? You're going hard on him tonight, huh?"

"I gotta go hard on him to remind your ass not to go there again."

"Girl, puhleeze, we're really over this time. I'm tired of his mankind bull."

"Oh, gosh, you're bringing it way back, huh?"

Tasha was referring to the one time I cheated on Brice. Right after he told me about his mankind theory. Even though Brice treated me like a sachet of diamonds, he still couldn't help cheating on me.

"It's in man's nature to cheat," he'd said.

"Man, as in male, or man, as in mankind?" I asked.

"Mankind. We aren't built as monogamous creatures. Humans are the only animals that try and we fail. But you know I don't love those other women. I come home to you every night, don't I?" he replied.

I guess I was lucky. Lucky to be the one he actually loved. Ha! So I tried his theory out for size.

For spite. See if he really meant that mankind bullshit.

Niles was the bartender at Suede. A lovely little spot that me and Tasha frequented Uptown. We'd take the Metro North to 125th Street every first Friday for their "Freak Out First Friday" event.

Niles wanted me bad. Secretly, I was feeling him too, but I never thought to cheat on my Brice. Why? He was good-looking, treated me like royalty and took care of me physically, emotionally and financially. But I couldn't go against the nature of mankind, right?

So, as always, Niles was hooking me and Tasha up with free drinks. He'd mix up things we'd never heard of and we'd be his testers. He knew we were into anything deceiving. Deceiving drinks tasted fruity and smooth but snuck up on your ass, and before you knew it, it was too late. You were fucked up!

He was looking great that night too. I knew Niles probably took home a different woman each night. Women fawned over him constantly. It was me throwing myself at him that night. Tasha warned me that Brice was going to kill me once he found out, but I explained to her that she was ignorant to the ways of mankind. I figured that if and when he found out about my wild night with Niles, he'd see how it was to be on the receiving end of the cheating.

Niles made us two key lime martinis. Then all three of us had a shot of SoCo and lime. Finally he finished us off with a Take a Cab—a drink that wasn't a Niles original, but he'd improved upon from the drink originally made popular in Miami Beach. That was it for me; I didn't want to drink too much. I wanted to remember that night.

Tasha was planning to go home with this dude she used to mess with back when we were still in high school. They were in the corner doing body shots of Patrón. That damn girl was blasted. But since we knew dude from way back in the day, I knew she was fine. She'd already told me when we first spotted him, she was fucking him that night.

Niles was cashing out and restocking the bar for the next night.

"You OK over there?" he asked me.

I was sitting at the end of the bar, nursing a glass of water.

Tasha had just stumbled out with back-in-the-day dude and slurred her good-byes to us.

"I'm good. Waiting for you," I sang, winking.

"Waiting for me?" He was used to drunken women making advances toward him. But his face couldn't contain his excitement about me being the woman that night.

"Go home," he said, still cheesing like a kid. He didn't think I was serious.

"Not tonight. I'm going home with you."

"Cassie, what about homeboy? What, you mad at him tonight? Y'all broke up or something?"

"No, but we have an open relationship. He

does his thing. I'm usually faithful, but tonight all that's going to change."

The alcohol had my head spinning. Had me feeling giddy, yet invincible. Sexy and sexual as hell.

Niles kept piddling around, doing his end-of-the-night routine. There were about five other people left in the club. Music had been turned off. Lights bright.

His smile.

His stupid, giddy smile was turning me on like crazy. His muscular arms were bulging out of his brown retro T-shirt with Bob Marley on the front. Jeans were loose. Not baggy. Low. Not sagging. Butt was nice. Not big. Not flat. Dreads. Neat. Shoulder-length. Dark brown. Almost black. Thick eyebrows. Wide nose. Full lips. Straight, white teeth.

"Drink this," he said, handing me a Red Bull. "You'll need some energy if you're serious about coming home with me tonight."

I ripped open the energy drink and guzzled down the first half.

Minutes later we were in his car headed to his house. The ride was short. I should've been nervous, but I was eager. Eager for revenge and eager to climb the walls in ecstasy with this fine man beside me.

We took the elevator to his fifth-floor apartment and didn't make it to the door before we kissed. Niles pressed me against the wall, holding my hands above my head, his erection pressing through his jeans, teasing my clitoris. We kissed like teenagers that didn't know any better. We kissed like there was no better pleasure in store. His hand invaded my shirt, dived under my bra and gently twisted my nipple. My moan explained how great it felt. One hand still over my head, pinned to the wall, the other now free to explore his body. I reached straight for the business. Just as thick as it was long. The perfect combination to get a chick strung out.

"Let's go inside," I whispered, eager to ride him into the next morning.

He let go of my breast and fumbled for his keys. Seconds later we were in his bedroom, standing before his bed. No music. No candles. No massages. Making love was not on the agenda that night. He threw me on the bed. Onto my stomach. My skirt landed on my lower back, exposing my ass. I tried to pull it back down. He pushed my hand away and planted his face into my ass. Both hands were cupping it while he licked the outside of my thong. I could've creamed on his face—if only he didn't stop. He stopped to peel my panties off with his teeth. Flipped me over. Pulled my skirt off and dived into my pussy. Licked. Sucked. Furiously. Gently. Hungrily.

I was drenched. His sheets were drenched. Only halfway there. He was still fully dressed and I still had my shirt and bra on.

He brought me to an orgasm two times with his mouth and kept going. Had to push him off me and take control of the situation. I was no pillow queen.

"Your turn, baby," I whispered. Voice hoarse from screaming obscenities at the Lord.

He stood in front of the bed. I spread my legs apart and pushed closer to the edge. Unbuckled his belt, unzipped his designer jeans. They dropped to the floor. I took his huge dick into my hands. Ogled it like it was a lobster dinner. Massaged it like it was a steak needing tenderizing. Licked it like salt off the side of a margarita. Sucked it like a Blow Pop.

"You might want to back up," he warned me, squeezing my shoulders tightly.

I was sure hoping he wasn't going to finish before we got to the best part. I pulled away from him and jerked him until the warm white cream of creation covered my hands.

I frowned, disappointed in his quick finish. But he fooled me. He remained erect and went to his dresser to get the condoms. Slid one right on and climbed on top of me.

"You don't need time to recuperate?" I asked, surprised that he had just come and was still erect and ready to go.

"You're funny, girl. You must not know 'bout me."

I cracked up for half a second and was pleasantly surprised when he entered me. I grabbed on to his dreads so he wouldn't push me through his headboard. Ran my hands through them, over and over again. Pulled them back so I could see the beautifully ugly faces of passion.

It was worth it. My one night of indiscretion with Niles. Well, it was worth it . . . until I got home the next day.

Brice was waiting for me when I got home at about ten o'clock the next morning. The ire in his eyes told me that I was in for it. But I was ready for a fight. Was ready to throw that mankind shit right up in his face. Teach him a lesson.

I was the one who learned a lesson that day, though. Men can dish, but they can't take it. What men do, women cannot. Men can't handle a fraction of the humiliation and betrayal of a cheating partner with half as much grace as a woman can.

So that was the first and last time I stepped out on Brice. At that point in life maintaining my posh lifestyle was more important than my dignity. So I kept my mouth shut when he stayed a night out. Didn't pry when he would ignore his cell phone rings late at night. Smiled at his feeble-ass lies. Played my position. Ringless wife. Concubine. Housekeeper. Whore. Therapist. Homie. Best friend.

I was soon pregnant with Mia, and things took a turn for the worse.

Chapter 15

Payton

It had been a helluva weekend. I had more drama in one weekend than I'd had all year. My old ass was worn out Monday morning at sports camp. The day dragged, but the kids didn't kill themselves playing dodgeball, so my job was done. As the director I spent half the day inside, enjoying the air conditioner, while the counselors baked in the sun with the kids.

I'd left a message first thing that morning for Dr. Weinstein concerning Keisha wanting to be able to see Alana. It was lunchtime and I still hadn't heard back from her. I'd given the main office's number and instructed the secretaries to page me on the intercom if she called.

I did have some messages on my cell phone, so over lunch I checked them. It was no surprise to me when I heard Summer's voice. She left only two messages this time. Crying. Boo-hooing actually. Asking, why? Begging to meet with me. I was unaffected by her waterworks this time. She'd got over on me too many times in the past by shedding tears. Not this time. I erased both messages and decided after work to go to the mall and get a new phone and a new number.

The painfully long day was over. Handled my business at the mall and headed home with my new phone. Alana had made us some spaghetti for dinner, so I didn't want to be late.

When I pulled around the corner and saw Summer sitting on my porch, I realized I wasn't dealing with the average breakup. *This one is going to be a bitch.*

I stopped two houses before mine and pulled over. Got out my new phone and called my home number. Alana picked right up.

"Hello."

"Hey, Sugar, it's me."

"What number you calling me from?" she wondered.

"Oh, I got a new phone. But listen. Did you know that Summer is at the house?"

"Yeah, I told that bitch she couldn't come in and she said that she'll just wait outside for you then."

"What did she say?"

Summer now noticed me parked on the side of the street. She stood up and arched her neck to see what I was doing.

Damn it.

"She ain't say nothing. I didn't give her a chance. She asked if you were home. I said no. She asked if she could come in and wait. I said no, and when she said she wasn't leaving, I slammed the door in her ugly-ass face."

"Alana, stop cursing," I reprimanded her. "Fuck!" I yelled, slamming my fist into the steering wheel.

"Oh, but listen to you!" she protested.

"First off, I'm grown, and furthermore, there's a friggin' psycho on my porch that I have to deal with."

Alana thought it was too funny.

"Want me to get rid of her? I'll fight her, Daddy. You know I don't care. I don't like her ass anyway. I'd love to slap her."

I didn't even think for a minute that Alana was kidding. I declined the tempting offer.

Summer left the porch just then and started toward me. I got out of the car. She wasn't going to punk me on my own block.

"Summer, whatchu doin' here?" I yelled, beating her to the punch.

"Well, you wouldn't call me back."

"So why didn't you take the hint? If I don't even want to talk to you over the phone, then why the hell do you think I wanna see you?"

"Take the hint? I'm not a fucking mind reader, Payton. I'm a person. With feelings. And I deserve better than this."

Damn, she is a person, I thought, *with feelings,* as she pointed out. And I was starting to feel like a real asshole. I'd never been this cold to a woman before. Not even one that deserved it. I mean, I guess I was over the comment she made about

Alana. I knew she just said it to hurt my feelings. She wanted to hurt my feelings because I'd hurt hers.

I wasn't responding. Couldn't even look her in the face. Why the hell was I acting like this?

She didn't keep arguing. Just stood there. Just stood there looking pitiful and lonely. She looked beautiful that day. But her baseball cap was concealing half her face. She was probably trying to hide her eyes swollen from days of crying.

She stared at me intensely. Searching my eyes for a sign that I cared.

"Summer," I finally answered, "why are you doing this? You know things weren't good between us. We should just cut our losses now. Let's not waste any more of each other's time," I offered in a soft tone.

"Look," she said, seeming to cheer up momentarily. She ripped off the baseball cap. "I cut my hair back off 'cause I know that's how you like it."

What am I dealing with here? I obviously had to handle her with kid gloves because she'd gone a little cuckoo.

"It looks nice, Summer. Real nice. But that's not going to make me wanna be back together with you."

We were standing about three feet apart. The air was still. Sun was setting. Cars were whizzing by in the distance. The silence was nerve-racking. I didn't know what else to say, but for some reason I couldn't walk away. She wasn't talking. Just standing there, looking like a lost pet.

She stepped forward.

I stepped back.

She stopped suddenly before me.

"Why are you doing this to me, Payton?" she begged again.

I wasn't prepared to answer that question. Not at all.

She started crying. First very quietly.

I stood there, feeling like the biggest jerk in the world.

What had she done that was so bad? Why did she have to pay for a promise I made to Keisha? Why couldn't she and Alana just get along? Then maybe she and I would stand a chance.

She lowered her head, ashamed of the emotions she could no longer restrain. Her cries grew louder, but she wouldn't look up. Her shoulders were slumped. She was defeated.

I stepped one step closer to her. Pondered giving her a hug. Rubbing her back. Letting her know everything was going to be OK. Then thought wiser of it. *She'll read too much into it,* I decided.

She finally raised her head. We were standing arm's length apart now. We were close enough that I could smell her Obsession. She looked at me and we locked eyes for a moment, and she lowered her head again. I crumbled. I reached in and embraced her.

"I love you, Payton. That's all. I just love you."

I thought I heard myself say it back to her, but the bright look in her eye, when she finally looked back into my face, let me know that I'd said it for sure.

Damn. I knew immediately that I didn't totally mean it, but I got caught up in the moment. Wanted to make her feel better.

She reached up and pressed her soft lips into mine. Her mouth parted and my tongue entered on cue. She squeezed me tight and we kissed like it was the last time we'd see each other. It was familiar. Felt good. The best I'd felt since the night we'd broken up.

We finally broke it up. My heavy breathing let her know that I wanted more. Didn't want this to end at kissing.

Summer felt confident enough to now look into my eyes. She even smiled. She'd won.

Women are the fucking devil.

"Can I come inside?" she whispered, knowing damn well I was in no position to decline.

Once again I didn't speak.

Just took her hand and led her down my street, then into my house.

Chapter 16

Cassie

I took a half day earlier this week to go to my gynecologist appointment.

It was only a couple blocks away and I ended up being there for about half an hour, but my job didn't need to know all that. My doctor did a routine Pap smear and I told her to run the gamut of tests on me, including any STDs and pregnancy.

By two o'clock I had the rest of the day to myself. I decided to surprise Mia by picking her up from camp early and taking her to get some ice cream. We were sitting out on the benches at Dairy Queen on Summer Street when my phone rang. It was Brice.

"Hello," I answered, annoyed. Shoot, I was trying to spend quality time with my daughter. My daughter.

"Look," he began, foregoing any greeting or slight pleasantry, "I'm going out of town, got a couple gigs lined up on the West Coast, and I was wondering if I could get Mia for a couple days. I'm leaving Friday."

"Sure," I agreed. I refused to be one of the spiteful baby-mamas. "When do you want me to bring her by?"

"Is that my daddy?" Mia wondered as her face lit up like a lottery winner.

"Yes, baby," I told her.

"Can she come by tonight? I can drop her back off on Wednesday."

"And you'll bring her back and forth to camp every day?"

"Yes, Cassie."

We agreed that I'd bring her over that evening right before her bedtime.

Shit, I could use a little time to myself. My mind was already racing, thinking of the things I wanted to do while Mia was away.

I dropped Mia off around seven that night. She was sad to see me go, but she wasn't that damn sad. When her dad opened the door, she sprinted into his arms and squealed, "Daddy!"

Brice didn't say a damn word to me. *Well, to hell with you too.* I turned on my heels and was out. *I think I'll call out sick tomorrow from work*, I thought. And maybe the next day too. Maybe even the rest of the week. I'll just tell them the doctor gave me some bad news and I need the rest of the week off. Hell, they would be all right without me. With that switchboard, receptionists were as disposable as a piece of gum.

First thing I did was call Tasha. She was always down to act a fool with me.

"I'm 'bout to put Freesia in the bed, so come on over," she said.

"All right, I'll bring some champagne. You got the 'chief'?" I asked her, hinting at our code word for marijuana.

We didn't smoke weed often. Hardly ever really, but I would say a good four times a year we'd get lifted.

"Not yet, but I'll run to the corner as soon as you get here to cop some."

I stopped back at my apartment to get a change of clothes and some toiletries. Then went to the liquor store and bought some middle-of-the-road champagne and a bottle of Peachtree to mix with it to make it sweeter. I knew that I would be in no condition to drive myself back home after getting tipsy and high with Tasha all night.

Freesia was knocked out by the time I arrived, around 8:30 P.M. Tasha ran out and copped the weed. From only God knows who—she kept the good connection.

We went out on her balcony. The air was dense and still. It was the perfect spot to get lifted— Freesia couldn't smell anything and it had glass doors so we could see her approaching if she woke up in the middle of the night.

I rolled it up like a professional. Licked the

edges of the blunt to seal it together and we lit it up.

Two blunts and three glasses of Peachtree-infused champagne later, we were lit.

"Girl, please promise it's over between you and Brice this time. He ain't shit, girl."

"I wouldn't say all that now. He's a good father, Tash. And he's a good guy. He's just not ready to settle down."

"He's a nasty-ass dog!" she yelled, sharing my anguish over the years wasted on him. "You keep trying to make him out as someone with just loyalty issues. He's disrespectful, he's possessive. Girl, open you're eyes. He ain't shit!"

"Why you being so hard on him all of a sudden?" I wondered.

She'd always been there for me through everything I'd been through over the years with Brice. Not once had she lashed out so angrily against him, though.

"Look. I just don't want to see you wasting your best years on his tired ass. It's not going to work—you've given it all you can give. Cut his ass off now and move on. I'm tired of hearing you crying over him and shit. You're getting pitiful."

"Pitiful?"

That stung. Like hell. Because I'd been thinking the past few days, and although I thought I was in control of me and Brice's little "arrangement," it did seem desperate and, well . . . pitiful.

"Yes, pi-ti-ful. And what?" she challenged.

Tasha stood up and propped both hands on her hips, daring me.

"Sit your ass down," I warned. "All right, all right. I know you're just looking out for me. I feel you," I told her.

"I love you, girl," she slurred, eyes tearing.

"I love you too," I returned. I stood up and hugged her.

We both started to cry on the spot.

When we finally released one another, Tasha made the drunk dial. She called Damon.

Our emotional exchange ended just like that. That's how it was when we were high. One minute we'd be cursing each other out. Crying the next. And seconds later cracking up over absolutely nothing at all.

It wasn't the first time Tasha called Damon since Saturday night, but in her altered state of mind, she just *had* to speak to him at that moment.

"C'mon, Tash," I slurred. "It's supposed to be a girls' night."

"I'm only going to be a minute," she insisted. "Lemme go get my phone."

She skipped into the apartment, yelling back, "I'ma order a pizza and some wings too while I'm in here. I'm hungry."

It was hotter than a bitch outside. My skin was moist and sticky. I was dizzy. Wide awake, but my eyes were closed tight. Couldn't keep them open. Stomach felt empty. The pizza was sounding real good.

Tasha came flying back onto the balcony a few minutes later. I rolled my head toward her in slow motion.

"Why the hell you making all that noise, girl? You're going to wake up Free!"

"Whatever. Look, I told Damon to come over."

"What!" I yelled, my eyes snapping open now.

"No, it's not even like that. He's going to bring that cutie, Payton, too."

"Tasha," I whined.

"What?"

"First of all, I look like shit. I'm drunk as hell. And I told you that I am not trying to get caught up in no one else right now. I can't believe this—"

Tasha cut me off. "Look, Damon said he would call Payton. There's no guarantees, OK?"

"Tasha, Freesia's in the other room."

"And?"

"And? And what if she gets up?"

"Look, *Mama gotta live too, OK?*"

She stared at me. I tried not to crack a smile, but we both laughed uncontrollably at her last line. It was what the mother from *Baby Boy* said to Jody about her thugged-out boyfriend: "Momma gotta live too."

When we were finally able to stop laughing, she poured me another cup of champagne and Peachtree. In true best-friend fashion she passed my already-over-the-limit ass another drink and poured herself one too.

"Look, just entertain Payton for about half an

hour, forty-five minutes, while Damon and I handle some biz in my bedroom, and that's it."

"Tasha!"

"What?" she said, looking all innocent.

"You're not fucking him."

"When . . . yes, I am!"

"When . . . no, you're not," I protested.

"Watch," she said with confidence.

Chapter 17

Payton

Alana was heated when she saw Summer follow me into the house. But before the madness started, I noticed how much effort Alana had put into making dinner. She'd set the table with our good plates, instead of the paper plates we usually use. She'd even had candles lit. I smelled the garlic wafting from the oven. The spaghetti was on the table in serving bowls.

Then I felt like an ass for ruining the evening Alana had planned for us by bringing Summer in the house. I immediately felt resentment toward her again. Once again she had come between me and my daughter.

"Daddy!" Alana screamed when she saw Summer. "What is she doing in here?"

"Baby, look. I'm sorry," I told her. "Summer and I just have some things to talk about, OK? Can I take a rain check on dinner?"

I looked down at my hardwood floors. I couldn't look either of them in the eye. Torn.

I couldn't at that point ask Summer to leave,

and I knew I couldn't sit down with Summer and eat the dinner Alana had prepared. Alana would spit nails across the room in anger.

"Daddy?" Alana yelled again, looking me up and down. I know what she expected me to do. I know what Summer expected too.

But before I could say anything—make any kind of decision—Alana stormed off, cursing and calling Summer all kind of expletives.

Summer stormed up the stairs. I followed Alana into the kitchen. She was tossing the salad she'd made—and the bowl she made it in—into the trash.

"C'mon, Sugar, don't do that. Just give me twenty minutes and I'll be right down. We'll have dinner together."

I grabbed her by the arm and she drew back with force.

"Don't you fucking touch me. You are so weak. Why is she here? Didn't you say you don't want her ass anymore? How can you stand me up after I spent all day trying to do something nice for you?"

She was bawling and gasping for air. I was stunned. She was her evil twin again—the one I'd met in Dr. Weinstein's office. She'd never, ever spoken to me like that before.

She was frantically pacing around the kitchen, throwing away just about everything in anger.

"Fine! I'm outta here. Spending the night at Missy's tonight. You have fun with your ugly-ass whore upstairs."

Made no sense for me to apologize and

convince her to stay. I tried, but she had rushed past me and slammed the door behind her before I knew it.

What the hell just happened?

I knew she'd be upset, but damn. It made me wonder more about this Parker kid and what role he was playing in Alana's new, uncontrollable anger. I felt bad. Ashamed that I let Summer bamboozle me into flaking out on Alana's dinner plans for us.

I wasn't too worried about Alana leaving. After all she was damn near an adult and pretty responsible. I trusted that she was going to her best friend Missy's house, like she said. And it was only a ten-minute walk away. Plus, it was better if she was that mad to get out and cool down. Now I just had to worry about the mess I had upstairs waiting for me. I'd been on a four-day roller coaster and I was ready to get the fuck off!

My mind was made up. I had to tell Summer to leave. Why did I kiss her in the first place? Alana was already gone. Her feelings were already hurt. Too late to fix that, but I just didn't feel like the drama Summer was sure to bring. When I opened the door to my bedroom, I realized the last thing on Summer's mind was drama. She was naked and provocatively sprawled out across my bed.

We made love. No, we fucked. Sweaty. "Fuck me harder. Harder. *Harder*" kind of fucking. I pulled her hair. She sank her teeth into my shoulders as I pounded her out. I choked her as

I hit it from behind. She creamed on me repeatedly. I loved it when her cum was thick and creamy. Thick, creamy and warm. Warm.

We used protection—although she tried hard to convince me that we didn't need it. I was at a weak moment, yes. But I wasn't that damn stupid. The condom went on and stayed on.

When we finally finished, I lay there and felt sick to my stomach. Disgusted at myself. Alana was right; I was weak. Summer rested her head on my chest and began rubbing her hand through my chest hair. It usually felt good. Endearing. At that moment, though, it only annoyed me and made me feel worse than I already did.

I was all messed up. I'd made my mind up to leave Summer alone. I'd vowed to be fully committed to Alana until I saw her off to school. And I'd just ruined both those goals in less than an hour. After I just witnessed Alana's meltdown a few days earlier, my mind was now racing wildly about her whereabouts and well-being. *What is Summer doing here?*

"Did you hear me, Payton?" Summer asked.

I hadn't even noticed she was talking.

"I said," she began, not waiting for me to answer her, "I think I should move in. I think I could be like a big sister to Alana. I really want to be a part of your family. Not just another woman that comes and goes."

Just as my head was about to explode, the phone rang and I rushed to answer it. She grabbed my arm. Her way of telling me to ignore the ringing phone. I needed a way out, though. Plus, it might've been Alana calling, so I had to pick up. It was Damon on the other end. He told me that he was heading to Tasha's house and wanted me to tag along. He explained that she and Cassie were having a girls' night, so the only way he'd be able to "get some" was if I accompanied him and entertained Cassie while he and Tasha did their thing.

Relieved to have a way out of this awkward situation with Summer, I agreed.

"All right, so meet me at the gas station by Exit 6 in about thirty minutes. She lives right around the corner from there," Damon told me before hanging up.

I placed the phone back on the nightstand. I turned to see Summer now sitting straight up with her hands folded over her chest. The defensive stance.

"Who was that?" she asked.

"Whoa, whoa, whoa. That's none of your business who that was."

Here we go again. I'd been in more altercations in the past four days than I'd been in the last year. I didn't give her a chance to get started. Not this time.

"Look, Summer, this whole night was a mistake. You shouldn't have come here. Now my daughter's pissed off at me and we're back to square one. I still don't want to be with you. I'm sorry, but this was all a big mistake."

"Payton, what are you saying? Why would you make love to me then?"

"I know, I know. I still haven't figured that one out yet either. But it shouldn't have happened. I'm really sorry we just did what we did. I was just going through the motions. Wasn't thinking. Maybe I just felt sorry for you."

There I'd said it. And I didn't stop.

"The honest truth is that I don't love you, Summer. I don't even like you that much anymore. I think you're a manipulative, self-centered, crass person."

She opened her mouth to talk shit, but I just tuned her out. Learned that skill early into our relationship. I hopped in the shower and locked the bathroom door behind me. Left her sitting on the bed with her arms folded. Minutes later I heard her knocking on the door, but I was drowning in my own thoughts. Eventually tuned out the violent thrusts she was imposing on my poor bathroom door too.

Took a quick shower, and when I opened my door, I wasn't surprised at all to see Summer was still there. Now crying.

"Payton, I'm sorry. I don't know what I did to spoil what we had, but I'm willing to work on this if you are," she offered.

I couldn't understand why she was so set on making our relationship work. I mean, we had no kids together. We hadn't been together that long. I hadn't done anything spectacular with her or to her. Which made her look completely insane for insisting that we work things out.

To pacify her, I said, "OK, Summer, we'll talk about it. Right now I just gotta go meet up with Damon, OK?"

I threw on some sweats and white T-shirt and tan Timberlands. Splashed a little Issey Miyake on and brushed my hair. Threw my wallet and cell phone in my pockets and was ready, with ten minutes left until I was due to meet Damon.

"You promise?" she asked, looking crushed.

"Promise what?" I asked, confused as to why she was even still here.

"Promise that we'll talk about things," she whined. Obviously disappointed that I couldn't remember something I told her only seconds before.

"Get dressed, go home and get some rest, Summer. I'll call you tomorrow."

"But why can't I just stay the night here?"

I thought hard about what I could say that wouldn't ignite another argument. I kept my real reasons to myself and told her that it wouldn't be a good idea if Alana came home tonight and saw her there. They might get to arguing and I wouldn't be around to referee.

She bought it. She got up and started getting dressed too. We headed out together and she kissed me on the cheek before we parted ways to our respective cars.

"Call me, Payton!" she yelled before ducking into her car.

"Uh-huh."

As soon as I got in, I called Alana's cell phone, and, surprisingly, she answered.

"Alana, I know I messed up tonight," I told her. "I'm sorry, baby."

"I accept your apology, Daddy. But my feelings are still hurt."

"I'll make it up to you, I promise."

Now that was a promise I intended to keep.

"OK then."

"So you spending the night out tonight?"

"Yeah, I'm at Missy's, Daddy. Remember, I told you?"

"Yeah. I just wanted to make sure, though. See you tomorrow?"

"I should be home tomorrow night. Me and Missy are going to the Trumbull Mall and then to Playland when it gets dark."

"All right. Love you."

"Love you too."

Chapter 18

Cassie

Damon and Payton arrived about an hour later. By then my high was gone and my belly was full. The only thing I felt like doing at that point was going to sleep. Tasha had taken a shower; so although her high was dwindling too, she was now rejuvenated.

With new clarity I posed a question, "Wait a minute, Tash. You don't mind these men that you barely know coming up in here while Free is here?"

"Girl, Free is a heavy sleeper. She'll never know someone was here."

"You know better than me, I guess," I replied with a shrug.

"Did you care when you were screwing Brice with Mia sleeping in the next room?"

"I guess not, but that was different. I know him well and he's her father, Tasha."

The doorbell buzzed and interrupted our morality debate.

I immediately felt nervous around Payton. He

looked surprisingly sexy in his sweatpants and smelled great too. We hugged like friends from way back.

"There's some leftover pizza in the kitchen and a couple wings left if y'all want some food," Tasha offered. "I'm about to mix up some daiquiris if anyone's interested."

Damn, my girl could party. The last thing on my mind was drinking some more. I was finally feeling the weight of the toxins we'd polluted ourselves with earlier being lifted. *Hmmm, but it would tame some of this nervousness that I was consumed with since seeing Payton again.*

It was a good nervous, though. I was happy to see him again.

It was almost ten by then, so I convinced myself that having another drink or two wouldn't be too bad.

We sat around for a few, sipping our cocktails. Light conversation. We talked about movies we'd recently seen, people we wanted to see in concert. Our opinions on restaurants around town.

Soon Tasha grabbed Damon's hand and excused herself.

"Just gonna show him something real quick. We'll be right back. Y'all talk amongst yourselves."

"You're a mess," I teased.

"And you know it," she replied with a wink.

The duo took off to the back of the house, toward Tasha's room.

That left Payton and me alone.

"Want a refill on your daiquiri?" I asked him.

"Sure, thanks."

Looked like there was something heavy on his mind.

"Everything OK?" I asked him when I returned with his drink.

"Hell no, everything ain't OK. My life is a mess right now," he confessed with a giggle.

"Wanna talk about it?" I asked.

Escaping from my reality and entering someone's misery sounded great at the moment.

"I'd normally pass. I'm a pretty private person and talking about things makes them too real sometimes, ya know? But I might be able to get some advice from you."

"Advice about women?" I asked. "That's my specialty," I said in an attempt to make it funny.

I sat back down beside him and tucked one of my legs underneath me, slightly leaning in toward him.

"So what's going on, Payt?"

"Payt. Right. Well, I just broke up with my girlfriend. We were together for about six months."

"That must really be hard for you. I'm sorry to hear that."

"No, it's not that hard. She's making it hard. I just want it to be over."

"And she's not having it, huh?" I chuckled.

"Not at all. We broke it off on Friday night and hadn't seen her until today when she showed up on my doorstep."

"Nuh-uh."

"Yeah, man. Pissed my daughter off 'cause

she had made dinner for us. Just too much extra for me."

"So what did you do? You let her in?"

His head dropped. He ran his hands across his goatee and smirked.

He let me know about the argument with his daughter and when he met his ex-girlfriend up in his bedroom—she was naked.

"Are you serious?" I squealed. "OK, see, now, that's when I would've called the cops."

"Yeah, that's Summer for you. She's bugged out like that. Won't take no for an answer."

"Are you saying you slept with her then?" I squealed again.

His hands once more ran across his perfectly trimmed goatee. He looked down in his lap. He answered my question with body language.

"Aw, man. Then I don't know who's worse. You or her?"

It was remarkable to me how he could see the faults in this woman. Know she was crazy. Know that he didn't want a relationship with her. Know that his daughter had prepared dinner for him. And yet still have sex with this woman. Maybe Brice had something going with his whole mankind idea.

"You are a *mess*. Seriously," I added with disgust.

He laughed. "Yes, I know. But feel me. These past couple days my emotions have been dribbled up and down like a damn basketball. Got punched in the face over a lovely young lady," he jabbed.

"Ha . . . ha," I responded.

"Na, but for real. Other than this Summer situation, there's some family issues I'm dealing with too. Deep issues that I know you don't want to hear about."

"Hey, I'm free until those two back there are done," I said, pointing toward Tasha's bedroom door, where she and Damon were doing the do.

Just when I thought I was going to get to know Payton on another level, he shut down.

"You know what? Let's talk about you. Tell me who Cassie is. Is that short for Cassandra?"

Not one to pry into people's business, I left it alone, but couldn't help but still wonder what kind of family problems he had going on. So we moved on to me.

"Yes. My name is Cassandra Stone."

"Stone!" he remarked. "You related to Angie Stone?"

"Angie from Custer Street?" I replied.

"Yeah, Angie from Custer Street. With the three kids?" he clarified.

"Yup, that's my cousin."

"Get outta here!" he said, slapping me playfully on my arm. "I used to kick it with Angie back in the day. That's your cousin?"

"That's what I said."

His glass was now empty and so was mine. So what the hell, I got up to refill both our glasses.

"Thank you," Payton said.

I returned back to my side of the love seat and tucked my leg back under me. Placed my left arm on the back of the couch and took a demure sip from my glass.

"Aw, man," he began again, "I haven't seen Angie in years. What a small-ass world," he remarked. "That's Stamford for you."

"Yeah, you right," I agreed. "OK, so back to me, right?"

"Yes, yes. Sorry, please continue, Ms. Stone."

Then he did this sexy thing with his mouth. Kinda smiled, I guess, but not really. More like he lifted the right corner up just a bit and let it fall, real slow.

"OK then," I said, snapping out of the gaze I had on his lips. "I'm twenty-seven. I'm a receptionist at a real estate developer's office downtown. Um. I have a daughter who's five. Her name is Mia. Brice is her father."

"OK, that all sounds good on paper. Can you introduce me to Cassie now?"

"What do you mean?" I asked, chuckling like a damn fool.

I don't like the way! He had me giddy for the second time in one day.

"OK. Tell me about your dream self. That person you would be if nothing ever got in your way."

My dream self, huh? Guess I never really thought of my dream self. Of course I had dreams, but after Mia was born, I just let them fade. Responsibility kicked in and silly dreams were kicked out.

"Well," I answered after some pondering, "I

would be a multiplatinum Mary J. Blige–status singer by now. With a big house—no, condo. A big condo for Mia and me. We'd never have to worry about money. Wait, not just Mia and me. I'd be married. Yes. Married. My husband would have a career he loved and would have plenty of time to spend with us. Yeah, that's my dream self—successful and happy."

"So you wanted to be a singer, huh?"

"Yeah, once. Well, still do really, but I am an 'old maid,' according to *them.*"

"Oh, forget them. They don't know nothing."

I took a moment to luxuriate in the thought of living in opulence. *My dream self.*

"You're really beautiful," he said out of nowhere. "I mean, really, really beautiful. And your short hair really sets you apart. And your body . . ." He paused. "You know what? I'ma stop because I think I'm crossing the line that I don't want to cross with you."

He was getting nervous now. Or maybe just tipsy. He didn't mean to admit his attraction to me.

"But," he continued, "for real, I think you can still make it. Don't let any industry-standards bullshit deter you. Break the mold."

I just blushed. Damn the alcohol and weed I'd smoked that night. Damn Payton for being so damned charming. Damn Tasha for inviting him and Damon over. Damn the fluttering feeling I was getting in the pit of my stomach. Needed some fresh air, so I suggested moving out to the balcony. He agreed.

"So what about your dream life?" I asked in return, once we reached outside.

"Hmmm. I'll think about that and let you know," he said, staring over the rail.

He'd shut back down. Why was he refusing to open up to me?

"Aw, that's really corny, man," I told him, punching him playfully in the arm.

"Yeah, I know. I know," he said, turning to face me. I faced him too.

He didn't budge, though. He wouldn't let me in. So we were caught in our first uncomfortable silence of the night.

And to make an uncomfortable moment even more uncomfortable, he reached in and kissed my lips. Softly. Next thing I knew, we were making out. And the term "making out" ain't even in my vocabulary. But I have no better way to describe it. Of course I'd been kissed before, but it was usually before or during sex. There was usually a hand or something else between my legs or up my shirt. But we just kissed. I draped my arm over his shoulder. A couple times he reached up and cupped my cheeks and pulled me closer into him, but that was it. No fondling, no fucking . . . just making out.

Chapter 19

Payton

It was almost 1:00 A.M. when Damon and I left Tasha's house. He had kissed—well, more than kissed—and was telling it all as we walked to my car. I didn't mention the kiss that Cassie and I shared. None of his damn business. Furthermore, I was starting to feel like a punk because I couldn't shake her scent from my nose, her taste from my mouth, the feeling of her soft hands against mine. Crickets were making love in the distance, letting out sounds of ecstasy for all to hear. There was a thick fog covering the ground. We could barely see two feet in front of us. The fog being the reason I didn't see my flattened tires until we were right up on the car.

"What the fuck?" I yelled, more like a question.

The front and rear tires of my car were completely flat.

"What the hell did you roll over, man?" Damon wondered.

"Yo, check the other side for me," I ordered.

Sure enough, the other two tires were flat too.

There was no way this was an accident. Someone had slashed my fucking tires.

"You think it was Summer?" Damon asked.

That was my immediate thought too, but it didn't seem to fit her style. If she'd done something for revenge, she wouldn't want to do it anonymously—she'd want me to know.

"C'mon, man," I said, waving his comments off. "She's crazy, but she's not violent."

"You're the one that said she was on your damn porch today, on some *Fatal Attraction*–type shit."

"Yeah, but—"

"Yeah, nothing. You better get that chick in check. She probably followed you here. Must've seen you and Cassie out on the balcony together," he suggested.

At that point I was beyond tired and wanted badly to get home. I paced back and forth, the light feeling Cassie had left me with was gone. I was a different man when I picked up the phone to call Summer. Was Damon right? Was I really caught up in a fatal attraction?

Not surprisingly, she picked up on the second ring.

"Summer, what the fuck is wrong with you?" I screamed, not giving her a chance to even say hello all the way.

"Excuse me?" she responded. "First of all, who are you talking to like that? Second of all, what are you talking about?"

"Don't you play stupid with me, Summer.

This was some really low shit. You can't be mad because I don't want you anymore. Move on!"

Damon found amusement in the conversation. He smiled widely as I continued my rampage.

"Summer, you slashed my tires. I should call the fucking cops on your deranged ass. Better yet, I should have one of my homegirls come pay you a visit."

"Pay me a visit? Payton, you're insane. I have nothing to do with your cheap-ass tires getting slashed, but I tell you what. I wish I did. Don't you ever call me with your bullshit again. And I wish you would send one of your little hood rat friends over here. I wish you would!"

I hung up in her ear. Didn't feeling like continuing the back-and-forth. I was convinced it was her trifling ass behind this stunt.

"So how we getting home, man?" Damon asked. "You know the cab number?"

Alana took cabs on rare occasions when one of her friends weren't available. I had Stamford Taxi programmed in my phone too.

I dialed the cab, and while we waited, Damon continued right where he left off about his and Tasha's night together. Sparing no details.

The cab arrived about twenty minutes later and I decided to leave my car parked on Tasha's street, buy some tires the next morning from Joe, my trusted mechanic, and Damon would help me put the new tires on after work. The driver dropped Damon off first and I finally arrived home to an empty house about 2:00 A.M.

I dragged myself into work the next morning, tired as an old dog. Thankfully, the campers had a field trip planned to Lake Quassy that day. I had plenty of dependable counselors, and some parents had even volunteered to chaperone, so I felt comfortable staying behind to catch up on some paperwork. Or so I told them. I was just tired and needed some time to myself to think about some things.

Right after the campers left, my office phone rang.

"Horizons Day Camp, Payton speaking," I answered.

The person hung up. I had a distinct feeling it was Summer playing games, but I refused to get worked up at work. I had a day to relax and I planned on taking advantage of it.

The phone rang again. It was Molly from Dr. Weinstein's office. Hearing her voice, and remembering the more prominent issue at hand, pushed the drama with Summer way back in my mind. I had to deal with impending divorce and whether or not to allow my soon-to-be-ex-wife of see our daughter again.

"Mr. Harris," she spoke softly, "I have Dr. Weinstein on the line. Returning your call. Can I transfer her through?"

I cleared my throat. Sat up straight in my chair.

"Hi, Molly," I replied. "Yes, please put her right through."

"Have a good day, Mr. Harris. Please hold on the line."

"Good morning, Mr. Harris," Dr. Weinstein's voice came over sternly in strong contrast to Molly's soft tone. "So have you thought about the birth control?"

I hadn't had a chance to think about that since Saturday when we were last in her office. It caught me off-guard.

"Uh, actually, no, I haven't. But I'll let you know on that."

It was times like this that I needed a woman to seek advice from. In my mind, hell no, I didn't want my daughter on birth control. If I were to ask Damon, I'm sure he'd double-down on the "hell no." But since Dr. Weinstein brought it up, maybe it was a good suggestion. I made a mental note to run it by Cassie the next time we spoke. Although we'd just met, she seemed pretty levelheaded. I thought she'd be the best person to consult with.

"I actually wanted to talk to you about something else today," I informed Dr. Weinstein.

I gave her the full details from the letter I received from Keisha.

"And I don't know whether it'll do her more harm than good by letting her see her mother again."

"You have to tell her," she told me. "Let her read the letter and come to her own conclusion. She may very well be so bitter about it all—she won't even want to see her. On the other hand, she might be touched and want more than anything to see her mother again. Alana's almost an adult now, so you have to respect that she is capable of making decisions about her life now."

"Hmmm," I hummed.

She continued, "Would you like to come into the office and have her read it here? Maybe I can help her work through her feelings."

I thought about it for a moment but decided that I'd like to be the one to help her through her feelings.

"No thanks, Dr. Weinstein. I'll take care of it at home, when the time is right. But thank you. I think telling her is the best thing for her too. I just wanted to be sure it was the best decision, you know?"

"I understand, Mr. Harris. Is there anything else?"

"I'll take the number for that gynecologist now. I'll have her set up an appointment and talk to her about birth control, maybe."

Dr. Weinstein gave me the gynecologist's information and we ended our conversation there.

I wasn't looking forward to laying this news on Alana, but finally I knew it was the right thing to do.

Bored and looking for a distraction from thoughts of Keisha's letter, Summer turning into a psycho, Alana possibly going on birth control and the nagging image of Cassie dancing through my head, I logged on to the Internet and went to SexyCTSingles.com.

Surprisingly, I had two messages already. All the shit on my mind was immediately pushed to the back burner as I excitedly clicked on the message entitled hey cutie. I wondered who this mystery woman could be.

The note was short: Cute pic, check out my

page and let's talk more. The message was left Sunday, the same night I'd created my profile. The second message was from last night, from the same sender, EvenSweeter. I clicked on EvenSweeter's second message. There was no subject line. I'm still waiting to hear from you, sexy. Have you seen my profile page yet?

My adrenaline rushed as I fumbled around, trying to figure out how to view her page. I didn't see a link to follow. I went to the home page and found a search field. In the field I typed in Even Sweeter, but thousands of results came back: Usually, when I ran into problems with the Internet, I'd just call up Alana. But I didn't want her knowing that I'd actually logged on to the Web site that I told her I didn't want to be bothered with in the first place. But after browsing through three or four pages of results, I gave up and called her.

"'Sup, Daddy?" she answered.

"Hey, Sugar, how you feeling today?"

"Better, it's all good. Me and Missy are just getting dressed. About to leave for the mall soon."

"Oh, OK," I said, stalling. Suddenly my embarrassment returned about being on a dating Web site and asking my daughter how to easily navigate through it.

"So what's up, Daddy?" she asked.

With growing anxiety over seeing EvenSweeter's profile page, I gave in again.

"All right, look. I'm on the silly Web site you made me sign up for, and someone actually sent me some messages and they want me to view their page, but I can't find her page. I tried searching for her by name, but it came back with thousands of names—"

"Daddy," she interrupted, "go back to your in-box."

"Shh," I told her. "Don't be having Missy and her desperate, nosey mother all in my business."

"Daddy! First of all, Ms. Davis is at work and Missy's in the shower. Can't nobody hear me. Anyways, go to the message she sent you."

"OK." I obeyed.

"Now just click on her name and it'll take you right to her page."

Damn, that easy?

"OK, I'm there. Thanks, Sugar."

EvenSweeter's page began loading.

"So it looks like you and Summer ain't working it out then, if you're on SexyCTSingles.com."

"Nope, not working it out. I know what I did last night hurt you, but I really just let her in because I felt bad for her. She was crying and carrying on. I was confused. But I promise something like that will never happen again."

"I forgive you, Daddy."

"All right, so you have a good time today. See you tonight."

"Love you."

"Love you."

My attention went right back to EvenSweeter's profile page. Her main photo was a shot of her legs. She was sitting down with her body turned to the left, with her legs crossed. Her legs were shapely, but I could tell she was a thin woman. Had a golden honey complexion. I mean, her legs were nice and all, but I wanted to see more—the rest of her body and definitely her face.

Her stats were single, no children, five-four, athletic build. So far, I wasn't turned off. But that was about all that was on her page. Very simple. Didn't tell or show much. Kinda like my page, simple and to the point. But at least I had a picture.

I went back to the message she'd sent me and pressed reply. Went to your page, wasn't much to see. Nice legs, though. Let's talk. Maybe I can see more pictures of you? What part of CT you from?

I pressed send and logged off. I'd officially stepped into the online dating scene. I never thought I'd see the day.

It was still very early and my campers weren't due back for several hours. So I sent an e-mail to my head counselors, telling them that I was leaving early to take care of some personal stuff and I'd see them all tomorrow morning.

I headed over to Joe's shop and bought some tires and went home to take a nap while I waited for Damon to take me back to my car and put the new tires on.

I read Keisha's letter again before heading to sleep and promised myself I'd let Alana read the letter that night. Not another day would go by.

Chapter 20

Cassie

First thing the next morning Tasha and Freesia left for work and camp, leaving me on the couch, groggy and with an agonizing headache. The sun was shining through Tasha's living room, irritating the hell out of me. I leaped up and snatched the curtains closed. I needed more sleep. Refusing to wake up with the same headache, I took a couple aspirin, ate a slice of dry toast and drank a tall glass of water before I crashed back on the couch.

I dreamt that Brice, Tasha and I were still singing together. I hadn't been plagued by my desire to sing since Johnny was a boy, figuratively not literally. I don't even know anyone named Johnny; it was just another one of those silly sayings me and Tasha had. "Since Johnny was a boy" meant several years had gone by. I guess it was all that talk about my dream life with Payton the night before that had me dreaming about our singing group back in the day.

Our group name was Indigo. Although we

called it a group, it was more like Brice was the lead singer and Tasha and I were his backup singers and dancers. Wherever we performed the women would scream and fawn over him and ignore the hell out of Tasha and me. We never really got anywhere with the group, though. Brice's head got too big. I was so busy running after him, trying to be his all, and Tasha was just tired of sharing the limelight with him.

So we disbanded Indigo and Brice decided to become a solo artist. Not to my surprise he's finally doing well and making a name for himself. He's actually gotten offers to get signed by a few small labels, but he's holding out for a deal with a major label. That was yet another reason why I knew he and I couldn't work this thing out. If he could never stay faithful even when he wasn't a star, he'd be a disaster once he blew up.

My dream was more like a flashback to the good ol' days. Tasha and Brice would fight like two Chihuahuas trapped in a paper bag. It was no fun for me being the buffer between those two. But I did manage to get a hell of a lot of laughs at their "yo' mama" and "you so ugly" jokes. But at the end of the day, we were family. Especially after a performance. We'd leave the stage and glide on this high. Gave us fulfillment like nothing else could. Those moments they'd forget any petty issues they'd been arguing about. I'd forget about the bitch-of-the-moment that Brice had cheated on me with. We were family.

Tasha and I bonded tightly over those two

years. So many times I would cry on her shoulder about something Brice had said, something Brice had done. She offered many times to loan me money so I could pack up and leave him. For some reason I could never let him go and I didn't want to be the one to break up Indigo either.

Tasha would say, "Girl, Brice will be successful with or without us. He's going to make it. You and I, we can become our own group instead of just his backup bitches. Indigo is my heart, but you're my sister. *You* come first and it's about time *you* put you first."

But in my dream everything was good. We were constantly on our performance high. Tasha and Brice got along. Brice never cheated. Life was harmonious, in my dream.

The phone rang and jarred me from my dream. My dream life. It was Tasha telling me to wake up and take my behind home. My head felt lighter, stomach felt a little queasy still, but in all I was ready to get home and start cleaning. I called the job from my cell phone and told them that I wouldn't be in. Although I have the personal time to take, my manager had an attitude. I could care less at this moment. I had more important things on my mind.

I cleaned when I was nervous. I cleaned when I was stressed. I used cleaning as a way to get my mind off things. That day I wanted to stop thinking about Payton and that kiss. Those kisses. Whatever.

His soft tongue left my lips tingling from its

touch. *Yum.* I wanted so much more the night before. I can't say that if he'd tried to take it to the next level that I would've stopped him. I felt alive again. Like for the first time I knew that someone other than Brice could take me there. Could make me feel that feeling. Not lustful like I felt with Niles, not pity or convenience like I felt with others. Just that feeling. That feeling like none other.

I shook my head. Shook him outta my thoughts. *Not going there,* I reminded myself.

I left Tasha's house at about noon and headed home with a strut in my step and a sexy switch in my hips.

When I reached home, the light on my phone was blinking, indicating I had a voice mail. It was my gynecologist saying she needed to speak to me as soon as possible.

Whenever I leave her office, she tells me that no news is good news. So I know that if I don't hear from her, then it's all good. I leaped to the phone and called her right back.

"Your Pap results came back abnormal. I need you to schedule an appointment to come back into the office. We're going to do a biopsy of your cervix to do further testing."

"What does that mean? Abnormal?"

"It could be nothing. But it could mean a lot more serious things. Things that should be caught and treated sooner rather than later. I'd rather not go into these possibilities right now. Don't want to scare you."

Too late!

"You're really scaring me, Dr. Wruth," I said, my voice quavering.

"I'm not going to sugarcoat this. Just come for the biopsy as soon as you can and we'll take it from there. Like I said, hopefully, it's nothing."

I didn't even know what a biopsy was, but she explained that she'd be cutting a tiny piece of my cervix off for testing. I told her that I'd taken the next few days off from work already, so my schedule was wide open. She tried again to convince me not to get too worked up before she transferred me to her receptionist to make my appointment. I was able to get in the next morning.

I threw on the soundtrack to *The Bodyguard* and blasted it as I cleaned my small apartment from top to bottom, inside and out. I forced Brice, Payton, Mia's sickle-cell anemia and my abnormal Pap results out the window and focused on my cleaning. Hard. In three hours my place was spotless.

My numb body went into autopilot for the rest of the night as I skipped dinner and fell asleep watching the news.

The next morning came quickly. Before I knew it, I was opening the door to Dr. Wruth's office.

The biopsy was done in the office—one snip and a quick burning cramp later, it was done.

"So we're going to send this off to the lab for testing. We'd usually just do another Pap smear and see if the results come back abnormal again before doing the biopsy. But with the prevalence and new awareness surrounding HPV, I want to move quickly to detect anything that may be harmful."

I'd heard of HPV of course. Seen the commercials about the vaccines that can be taken now to prevent getting the virus. But still I was ignorant to exactly what it was and how it was caused.

"Human papilloma virus is sexually transmitted. It's very common though. In fact, most people that are sexually active have had it at one point or another. Statistics show that three in four people that are sexually active have it. Some types manifest in genital warts, other types of HPV have no symptoms at all. But the most serious kind causes cancerous cells to grow on you cervix. So you can see why we wanted to do this biopsy right away."

Dr. Wruth was reciting the facts of HPV like a speech she'd delivered a million times before.

"So if the results come back positive, then you should tell your partner right away. If you're both treated, you won't be able to pass the same type of HPV back and forth. But, like I said yesterday, there may be no cause for alarm at all. Pap smear results come back abnormal all the time."

"Uh-huh." I swallowed.

"The good news though is that the HIV test came back negative, no other STDs came up and you're not pregnant. So as soon as we sort through the results of this biopsy you'll have a clean bill of health. Unless of course, you have HPV."

"So how soon will the results be back?" I asked.

"Few days, that's all. I'll give you a call as soon as the results come in."

I left, feeling like a cup half empty.

After strapping my seat belt on, and before starting up my car, I flipped open my phone to call Tasha. She wasn't at her desk, so I left her a message asking her to call me back.

Before I pulled out, I noticed a piece of paper stuck in my windshield. Looks like a flyer or advertisement.

I unstrapped my seat belt and got out of the car to get the note.

I impatiently unfolded the paper and read the red words out loud:

"Stay the FUCK away from my man."

Chapter 21

Payton

Got my car back on the road at about six o'clock that night. Picked up some Chinese food from Uncle Dai's and laid the spread out for us. I had spoken to Alana a few hours before and she planned to be home by seven o'clock the latest.

I sat at the kitchen table tapping my fingers against the table. The letter was folded up in my back pocket, burning a hole through my pants. My armpits were moist and I couldn't stop shaking my foot under the table. I hadn't felt this nervous since the night I got that mysterious call from Keisha.

Alana walked in, just before 7:00 P.M., and ran straight upstairs.

"Alana," I yelled from the kitchen. "I got some Chinese food for us. Come on down and eat."

"OK, Dad, just gimme a minute," she yelled back.

I jerked from my seat and raced to the fridge to grab a beer. Flipped open the lid and guzzled half of the contents in one gulp. *Breathe.*

"'Sup, Daddy?" she said, standing on her tip-toes to kiss my cheek.

"Hey, Sugar," I meekly replied.

"'Swrong withchu?" she wondered.

A laugh escaped my mouth and I looked at the floor. Ran my hands across my goatee and reached for my back pocket.

"Nothing's wrong. Um. I—I just have something to show you," I stuttered.

Alana grabbed a paper plate from the top of the microwave, a fork from the drawer and began opening the cartons of food.

"Ooooo, you got me some egg foo yung. Did you get some wings too, Daddy?"

"Yeah. Uh, yeah, it's all there. I know what you like."

I didn't know how to announce what was in my hand. Didn't have the right words to say to prepare her for it.

So I just stuck out my hand and told her, "Here."

"What's this?" she asked, placing her plate on the table and taking the letter from my hand.

Alana sat down, unfolded the letter and started to read. I guzzled the remaining half of my beer.

Her facial expression didn't change the entire time she read through the letter. When I saw her eyes stop moving back and forth across the page, I noticed she took a couple extra seconds to digest it all.

My eyes darted around the room. I was sure

I'd see her personality B come out and flip the script any second.

"Man, fuck her," she finally responded.

She balled the letter up and threw it across the room.

"Alana," I pleaded.

"Daddy. Stop. I don't want to see her and you can't make me."

She calmly picked up her fork and began eating.

I still hadn't made my plate. I was starving when I went to get the food, but my appetite was now gone.

She didn't look up. Just kept eating.

Was that it? I thought. She seemed to handle it well. Too well. Feeling slightly more at ease, I grabbed the container of shrimp fried rice and dug my fork into it.

The quietness between us would make a deaf man's ears ring.

"I cannot believe after all these years, that bitch thinks she can just write a fucking dumbass letter and expect me to want to see her! I will kill that bitch if I see her. Give her the damned divorce. She never deserved to be a Harris to begin with."

Oh, shit.

Alana stood up and pounded her fists against the table repeatedly. Her food spilled over on the floor. She didn't care or notice.

"Sugar—"

"No! Don't you say one word to defend her! She's a selfish bitch and I hope she dies! I was better off believing that someone raped and killed her."

Her eyes were instantly red and her face wet from crying. My eyes began welling up at the sight of her so hurt. She turned around and grabbed the chair behind her. Launched it across the room. Her nose was flared, chest heaving, her breathing labored.

"She hasn't done a thing for me. Not one thing! I got my first period without her. Bought my first bra without her. Did my own hair since I was ten. I never needed her for shit. And I don't need her now!"

"Where's your medicine, Sugar?"

I didn't know what to say or do, but I knew she needed to calm down.

"I'm not crazy, Daddy. Don't you treat me like that!" she screamed.

I jumped up and grabbed her in my arms. Hugged her.

"Sorry. Sorry. I didn't mean to say that," I explained. I wanted to kick myself for suggesting she needed medication.

Hugged her so tight that she couldn't move her upper body, so she started stomping her feet.

"Get off me!" she yelled, trying to wriggle out of my grip.

"I love you!" I yelled back. And I had never meant it more than right then.

She finally gave up the fight and buried her face into my chest, hugging me back. She took long, deliberate breaths.

"Daddy, why didn't she want me? What's wrong with me?"

The tears that had been welling up in my eyes now began to spill over, traveling down my cheeks and falling on her shoulders.

Again I didn't have the answer. Didn't want to say something stupid.

So I said once more, "I love you!"

The chair had hit the wall and knocked our portrait of the Last Supper off the wall. Shards of glass were on the counter, on the stove and on the floor. There was food spilled all over the floor and table.

We were standing amidst the mess Alana had created, holding on to each other like we were the last two people on earth.

She wailed for a few more minutes and I just couldn't let her go. Didn't want to let her go. Felt good being her support.

"I love you too," she finally replied, breaking the silence.

She loosened her grip from around me and I let finally let her go.

With swollen eyes she turned and left the kitchen.

"I'm going to bed early," she told me.

My head was spinning and I felt completely drained from Alana's emotional response to Keisha's letter.

The next thing I needed to do was call Keisha, I thought. But first I had to clean up the disaster in my kitchen. I knew Alana well enough to know she needed to be alone right then. She didn't deal well with being smothered when she was upset.

Nothing tore me apart more than to see Alana so upset. And this was the second day in a row that she'd hit the roof. Third time in four days.

I dragged my heavy body around the kitchen, carefully sorting through the glass and cleaning up the mess. Seems like it took hours. Each moment went by in slow motion. I located the crumbled letter and unfolded it. Quickly, feverishly, almost desperately, I grabbed the cordless phone off the wall and dialed the number written on the bottom.

She answered. The voice stank with familiarity. She sounded happy. Answered the phone with a smile. I could hear it in the way she said hello.

It all came back to me in a rush of anger. All the bad memories. Staying up for days, hoping she'd come home. Impatiently awaiting a phone call from the police station. Dragging baby Alana around town, begging for food from family. Finally getting a call from the police; the case had gone cold, she is presumed dead, they said. Missing work so often that I got fired. Having my whole life as I knew it crumble before my eyes. Felt like I'd just gotten hit on the back of the head with a bat. *Whomp!*

"Keisha," I replied, voice quavering. Scalding tears ran down my face. Wondered if she heard it in my voice. I was smoked!

"Yes, this is she," she answered, pissing me off with her cheeriness. My daughter and I were erupting like volcanoes over here, and there she was—all cheery and shit.

Felt like after I got hit with the bat in the back of my head, someone kicked me in the stomach and knocked the wind out of me. I opened my mouth to announce who I was, since she obviously didn't remember my voice, but nothing came out.

Frustrated and struck speechless, I hung up the phone.

I'm not ready for this.

Chapter 22

Cassie

I looked around to see if someone was watching me, waiting to see my reaction to the threatening note. There was an elderly couple walking down the street, holding hands. A lanky white man walking his dog and a Hispanic teenage girl walking by, pushing a baby stroller.

Who the hell left this note? Who the hell knows I was at my doctor's office? Have I been followed?

Sordid thoughts swam through my head, but I quickly came to the conclusion that it was one of Brice's groupies. She need not worry; I was too through with him.

I took the note back into the car with me and stuffed it into my purse. I had to show Tasha the note in person or she just wouldn't believe me!

The vibrating, ringing combination of my phone jarred me out of my state of shock. I jumped in my seat and grabbed the wheel, like I'd just heard gunshots ring through the air. The note obviously had me shook.

I snatched my phone quickly, figuring it was

Tasha calling me back. I just couldn't wait to tell her what had happened. But it was a number I didn't immediately recognize. The voice, however, I recognized immediately.

"Hello," I said in my most collected tone.

"Hey, Cassie, it's Brice."

I couldn't hold back.

"Brice, you better tell all your little groupies something. One of your friends just left me a threatening note on my car. My car, Brice! That means one of your bitches has been following me. You'd better get this shit in check and you better do it quickly, because I will not be a part of this high-school shit. You feel me?

"They need to understand that I don't want your ass. I'm just around because of Mia. And they need to just get used to me being around because we're tied together for life because of that little girl. I deserve more respect than this, Brice. You better check the bitch that's threatening me. She don't know me like that!"

I didn't realize how loud I was screaming until I was done and felt how quiet the car had gotten and the silence coming from the other line.

"You done?" he asked, unfazed by my tirade. "I can assure you that anyone I'm dealing with has more class than to do something like that. But I can listen to you yell about that another time. I thought you should know that Mia's having a pain crisis. Thought you might want to come be with her."

Immediately I felt small. Carrying on about

something that in the scheme of things wasn't that serious. My baby was in pain!

I hooked a tire-screeching U-turn and headed in the direction of Brice's house. I never could control my emotions very well when it came to Mia's sickle cell. And this time was no different. I bawled the whole ride there.

Once I arrived in front of Brice's house, I sat in the car and prayed. *Lord, please help my baby through this one. Take the pain from her and give it to me. I can handle it; she can't. She's only five, God. Please send her healing mercies. Give me the strength to be her rock, Lord. Amen.*

Brice had left the door open for me, so I sprinted right inside. Immediately I heard her crying upstairs. I took the stairs, two by two, and was in her room in just a few seconds.

She was pale. A thin layer of cold sweat covered her body. Even through the pain, her eyes lit up, if only for a moment, when I entered the room. Her mouth was open. Lips dry and chapped beyond belief.

"Mommy?" she asked.

"Baby, I'm here. I'm here, baby."

Kneeling by her side, I rubbed my hand across her forehead. Gingerly stroked her hair. Nothing I could do, but stay there. Let her feel my presence. And pray it would soon be over.

I saw him sitting in the corner, looking like a cornered wild animal. It had been years since he had to deal with one of her pain crises. He wasn't dealing well.

"Did you give her a folic acid vitamin today?" I asked. Not that it mattered, but I just felt like saying something to break the uneasy silence. I hasn't even said hello.

"Don't insult me," he answered.

Well, fuck it, I thought. We can just sit in silence, for all I care.

Mia was able to fall asleep soon after I arrived. Brice was sprawled across the chair. The same chair he'd been in since I first got there. He hadn't moved.

I crawled into the bed beside Mia, careful not to wake her. It was only early afternoon, but we'd all been through the spin cycle. I'd been through three times already that day. My sleep would be therapeutic and much needed.

The doorbell ringing jarred me out of my slumber. I jerked upright and looked around feverishly, not quite remembering where I was. Then I saw Mia sleeping to my right and was blasted back into my reality. Thank you, God, for letting her get some rest. There were times when rest didn't come at all for her when she was in pain.

Then I heard whispers coming from downstairs. Loud whispers. Like an argument that wasn't supposed to be heard. That didn't *want* to be heard.

For the first time I didn't care who the woman's voice belonged to. Didn't care what they were arguing about. That was until the voices went from a loud whisper to a soft yell. That's when

I realized that one of the voice belonged to Tasha. My friend Tasha. I shook my head from side to side. Back up. *My* friend Tasha is downstairs arguing with my ex-fiancé, baby-daddy, whatever. Something smelled like shit and it wasn't me or Mia!

I tiptoed out of the bedroom and down the hallway, spying over the rail that overlooked the foyer below. Sure enough, it was Tasha.

"No, we need to tell her now," she demanded. I could now clearly hear what they were saying.

"Tell me what?" I yelled from overhead, unable to spy a moment longer. I didn't plan to give myself up so quickly, but I needed to know what the hell was going on. Like yesterday! For that moment I forgot to keep quiet for my sick baby's sake.

"Tell me what? Huh? Tasha, what are you doing here?" I asked, barreling down the stairs. With the day I'd had, I was ready to swing first and ask questions later.

"Tell her," Brice said, arms folded across his chest, defiantly.

"No, you tell her," she barked back.

I was standing between them, waiting for answers. In a moment I didn't recognize my best friend. She was being a coward. My outspoken, loudmouthed best friend, who never gave a damn what nobody thought, wouldn't talk. Couldn't talk.

"Somebody better tell me something right now."

I heard Mia softly calling for me from the

distance. I'd awakened her with my carrying-on. The mother in me wanted to run back up the stairs and cuddle my daughter. But the woman in me needed to know what was going on.

"Look, we wanted to tell you about this when the time was right," Brice started.

"Bullshit," Tasha fired. "He's lying!"

"But Tasha wanted to keep it a secret."

"You lying son of a bitch!" she yelled, stepping into his face. "Tell her the truth!" she cried, pointing at me.

"Mommy," I heard again in the distance. Brice stared upstairs toward Mia's room. The father in him wanted to run upstairs and tend to his daughter. But the man in him wanted to play this twisted game with me and Tasha's head.

"Cassie," Brice continued, "Tasha and I slept together."

When I came to, Tasha was gone and Brice was waving a paper plate over my wet face.

"You OK? You just fell out!" he yelled, looking frantic.

Damn, I knew I'd been under a lot of stress lately, but I guess not having eaten anything that day took me out. When Brice told me he'd slept with my best friend, my body just couldn't handle another thing. I might have checked out for a minute, but I didn't forget the information that was just slapped on me.

"Don't you fucking touch me!" I yelled in disgust.

"Oh, gosh, lemme explain, Cassie."

"You know what? This is why I'm done with your ass. So I don't have to hear another one of your lame-ass excuses ever again. Save your breath!"

I jumped up from where I lay and almost fell right back down. The room was spinning and my eyes went out of focus for a second. I stumbled but quickly recovered and charged up the stairs.

"Cassie!" Brice yelled after me, following me up the stairs.

Halfway to the top I turned around to scold him.

"You don't owe me anything."

Mia was crying. I'm sure she didn't understand what was going on, but she knew her parents were upset.

"Do you feel better, sweetie?" I asked, grabbing her clothes so I could put them on her.

"My legs, Mommy," she whined.

"Cassie," Brice whispered, standing behind me, "don't leave with her now. Let her rest here until she feels better."

"C'mon, honey bunch. Lift up so I can put your shirt on," I directed Mia, ignoring Brice.

"Just let me explain," he begged.

"You don't owe me a damn thing," I told him again.

I finished dressing Mia and we left in a haste. Brice was carrying on, but I tuned him out. Had to get outta there. Didn't want to make a scene in front of Mia. And Lord knows, there was a scene brewing inside me!

Mia softly whimpered the whole way home. Unbeknownst to her, so did I.

Chapter 23

Payton

When the phone rang back not even two minutes later, I swallowed my fear, manned up and answered. From the caller ID I could see it was Keisha phoning back.

"Hello," I answered, clearing my throat.

"Payton?" Keisha asked.

"Uh, yeah."

"So I'm assuming that you got my letter?"

"Uh-huh."

"Don't you have anything to say? Go 'head, let me have it," she humbly stated.

"Keisha, man, look, it's been so long. It doesn't even matter what I want to say to you right now. I'm glad you're alive and happy, that's all."

"So . . . when can I come see Sugar?"

"Na, that's not happening. She doesn't want to see you, and to be honest, you really don't deserve to see her, Keisha. I mean, you went on and got better. Started another family. C'mon, man, how do you think that makes her feel?"

"I—I guess I can't blame her," she whispered.

The cheeriness was now knocked out of her. "But I'm saved now. I'm a Christian. Just trying to correct the mistakes that I made in the past."

"Well, I'm sorry that we can't help you clear your conscience, but it is what it is. And for the other thing."

"The divorce?"

"Yes, the divorce. Do you have the paperwork ready?"

"Just need you to sign," she said sullenly. "My family and I are actually going to be heading to the Arena at Harbor Yard to see *Disney on Ice* tomorrow night. You think we can meet up and get them signed then?"

"Can't you just put them in the mail? I'll sign them and mail 'em back to you."

"I don't want to drag this out anymore, Payton. Just want to get on with my new life."

"Yeah, you know what? Me too," I replied indignantly. "Tomorrow works."

"I hear y'all living in your mom's old house now. So how 'bout I meet you at the Dunkin' Donuts on Strawberry Hill?"

"Excuse me, but how the hell did you know where I was living?"

"You weren't the only one I sent a letter to. I sent one to my sisters and my mother too. They told me that they see Sugar around town from time to time, but she hasn't been very friendly toward them. Said they see you too, sometimes."

"Can you blame her? Half the time we see them, they're begging for money or food. I made it a point to keep them away from Alana as much as possible."

"That's my family. And her family, Payton."

"Ha-ha!" I yelped. "That's where you're wrong. I am her family. Just me."

Keisha chuckled, like what I said was cute to her. And it annoyed the shit out of me, but I didn't feel like getting into it with her. Couldn't let her know that I cared enough about her to get upset.

But I was smoked. Not sad anymore. I think if we were face-to-face, I would've strangled her. She wasn't even talking sideways or anything. I just came to the realization that I hated her for what she'd done to me and wanted to take her last breath for the damage she'd done to Alana.

We agreed to meet at Dunkin' Donuts at 5:30 P.M. the next day. I abruptly hung up the phone on her, once the meeting time was set.

The night felt endlessly long, but it was only about nine o'clcok by the time I'd cleaned up the kitchen and hung up with Keisha. Slowly I ascended the stairs to my room, listening for sounds coming from Alana's room. All I heard was the quiet hum of the television.

Too wound-up to relax, I plopped onto my bed and put both palms on my throbbing head. With my left leg I kicked the door closed with a slam.

Unbelievably, I had a strong urge to talk to Cassie. Damon was my dude, but I was too vulnerable at that moment. I didn't want to be a bitch in front of my boy. I fought with myself for a few minutes and decided to just give her a call. Maybe she'd lift my spirits with that sweet voice of hers and that sense of humor.

But when she answered the phone, she sounded awful.

"Hey, Payt," she whispered. "Just put Mia to bed finally. She's not feeling too well today."

"Oh, OK, if it's not a good time, I can catch up with you later then," I rushed out nervously.

"No! It's OK," she rushed back. "I think I need someone to talk to."

"Yeah, me too. Today has been one for the record books."

"Ha! You too, huh? I don't know what I did wrong, but that bitch Karma found me today and kicked my ass!"

"Can I see you tonight?" I blurted out, not afraid of rejection. Usually, I wouldn't have put myself out there like that, but I wanted to see her that night. Badly.

She accepted just as quickly as I asked. Even though after hearing her voice I suddenly couldn't wait to see her, I took a shower and changed my clothes before leaving.

Peeped in on Alana to let her know I was heading out, but she was sound asleep. I followed the directions Cassie gave me and was at her house in fifteen minutes. She looked worried, but she smelled freshly showered when I reached down to hug her. She smelled like lavender and vanilla. I held her a moment longer and put my face in her neck and breathed.

We stood in her doorway, taking each other in. Felt good to be out of my crazy reality.

"Come and have a seat," she said, heading toward her living room. "Welcome to the palace," she joked.

She was wearing pink boy shorts and a white tank top, no bra, with flip-flops. Pretty feet. Sexy toes painted soft pink. No makeup, her short hair still wet from the shower. And she was still beautiful.

We sat on her love seat. Got déjà vu. Was reminded of a couple nights before, when we were kissing on Tasha's couch. Touched her hand. She looked into my eyes. So much was behind those eyes. They had a story to tell. But not that night. When I touched her hand, she moved closer to me.

"Wanna talk?" she asked.

"Not now. Let's just enjoy this peace."

Her eyes stayed glued to mine. It seemed like the natural thing to do at the moment, so I kissed her. Her lips softer than the first time. Tongue sweeter. She moved closer to me and soon our bodies were pressed together. Her full breasts pressed against me. Soft. Then I got hard. Without notice she reached down and massaged my erection through my jeans. Her forwardness was unexpected. Threw me off my game a little bit. It wasn't what I came over for, but if she was taking it there, then I was gonna go along for the ride.

Our soft kisses became intense, like we depended on each other's oxygen to survive. She now had a firm grip on my erection, so I went for her breast. Squeezed it gently through her shirt. It fit perfectly—just a handful, that's all I needed. She responded by unhanding me and grabbing the sides of my face while she pushed her tongue roughly into my mouth. I let that be my invitation to go under her shirt and feel her soft skin.

Cassie straddled me, pulled her shirt over her head and threw it across the room. Her body was perfect, even with the few stretch marks. It was so quiet in her apartment. The only noise was our bated breath.

"Let's go in my room," she announced.

She crawled off the couch and reached down for my hand. I grabbed her hand and waddled behind her, admiring the smooth skin of her bare back and the cusp of her ass falling out of her boy shorts.

We passed her daughter's room and I heard the slight wheeze of a good night's sleep. A brief feeling of guilt ran through me. I hadn't even met her daughter, yet I was about to make love to her mother in the next room.

That moment quickly passed when Cassie closed her bedroom door behind us and pushed me down on her bed.

She reached in a drawer next to her bed and threw some condoms on the bed. I pulled my shirt off and started unbuckling my jeans, while she took her shorts off and stood over.

She hungrily pulled off my jeans and climbed on top of me, shoving her left breast into my mouth. I gladly pleasured her nipples with my tongue and delivered a few light bites. Her moans let me know she loved the biting.

I grabbed her ass and she began grinding slowly over my erection, not taking me inside her, though. Teasing me.

She removed her breasts from my mouth and returned the favor by slowly massaging my nipples with her tongue. But only for a moment before she traveled down my love line to formally introduce herself to my penis for the first time.

She greeted "him" with a kiss. A long, wet kiss. Who'da known it was the first time they'd met? You'da thought they were old lovers who hadn't seen each other in ages. She kissed him like she missed "him". Then she lost it on me.

Took me in and out of her mouth a thousand times as I writhed in ecstasy. Her hands and mouth moved in a sweet, opposing rhythm that brought me to a level of carnal insanity that I didn't dare go to just yet. Cassie was no rookie.

I had to take over; she was about to punk the shit out of me. And I didn't want to finish early and not be able to please her back.

I grabbed her shoulders and gingerly led her away from my erection, just in time.

Stayed on my back and lifted her up over my head. I couldn't wait to feel her melt in my mouth like cotton candy. She grabbed the headboard and held on with conviction as I placed her on my face.

Soon I felt her juices dripping down the sides of my face. Then she got loud. Really loud. Her screams knocked me out of my groove. I got nervous that she'd wake up her daughter. Grabbing her by the waist, I lifted her up and placed her on my stomach while I maneuvered to put one of the condoms on.

With the protection in place, I pushed her on top of me and she slid down slowly. My toes curled up. *Oh, God.*

Cassie squealed as she slowly worked her way down my shaft. She leaned forward and took my tongue into hers again and began moving her hips in a circular motion. *Yup, no rookie,* I thought again.

She was in euphoria on top of me. I was enjoying her on top so much that switching positions didn't even cross my mind. Cassie's movements were deliberate and measured. I found myself craving the next stroke.

The August heat had our bodies slick with perspiration and barely able to breathe.

At just the precise moment she arched her perfect back and threw her head back and let out a muffled scream as her lower body jerked uncontrollably. Her sharp movements quickly brought me to my own special place along with her. We quietly sang the same song while squeezing one another's hands.

"Shit," she whispered, and she lethargically climbed off me.

When the electricity in the air settled, I felt uncomfortable and unsure. Hoped that this wasn't a mistake. We still barely knew each other. I didn't want another Summer on my hands. We both lay there, staring at the ceiling, speechless. The sex was incredible. The moment we shared special. I didn't want to ruin it with bringing up what I'd hoped to talk to her about that night. Maybe another time. No need to burden her with my mess; I was sure she had her own.

Chapter 24

Cassie

I wrestled with myself about whether or not to open up to Payton about Mia's sickness, not to mention my own, as well as the nonsense I was going through with Brice and Tasha. We lay side by side after making the most incredible love, but I didn't know how to read his silence. When we spoke on the phone, we both had said we had issues we wanted to get off our chests, but I wanted badly for him to open up first. I knew if I slammed him with my issues, he'd want to talk about them all night and he'd close right up when it was his turn.

Wanted to ask him what he was going through, but I didn't want to pry where he hadn't invited me. So we lay there for almost an hour; neither of us said a word. But a thousand thoughts and emotions ran rampant in my mind. Funny how we could share our bodies so freely but couldn't be there for each other in a time of need.

I couldn't sleep if I wanted. I wanted to bask in the moment. I mean, the sex was so on point. Wanted Payton to open up to me. Bond through sharing our drama. But with Mia feeling a little better, the thing most heavily on my mind was Tasha sleeping with Brice.

What the hell? Talk about blindsided! That would explain her little act of hating him so much, I guess. Great diversion tactic. Since cutting Brice off and meaning it, cutting her off would be easy, I reasoned. I just found it so sinister that she could be so phony. Keep me so close, knowing that she was betraying me. I considered her my sister; we were closer than blood.

I fought back tears, only because I was sharing my bed with Payton. If he hadn't been there, I'm sure my pillow would've been soaked with tears.

For Payton, rest wouldn't come either. I turned to him and began rubbing his chest hair.

"You OK?" I asked.

"I'll be a'ight," he whispered. "But I should get out of here. You're playing hooky this week, but I still gotta make it to work tomorrow," he joked. "And I don't think it's too cool if Mia gets up and sees me here, ya know?"

"No, of course. You two should meet before she sees you climbing out of my bed," I retorted, laughing.

Payton slowly climbed out of my bed and crept around the room, putting his clothes back on. I enjoyed watching him. His body was sculpted perfectly. His placid penis still hung low, proudly. Peering at his penis allowed me to briefly bask in our lovemaking. Briefly.

Fully dressed, he bent over to kiss me on the forehead. *The forehead?* Told me he'd call me.

"And I really want to talk to you, Cassie. I do. Let's definitely get together sometime this week, OK? I want to know what's been bothering you. Tell you a few things going on in my sorry life too, OK?"

"OK," I agreed.

Mia stayed home with me the next day. She insisted that she felt better and wanted to go to camp; they were going on a field trip to Playland. But I didn't trust that she was completely ok by then. Maybe there was some selfish intentions too—I didn't want to be alone with my thoughts that day. Taking care of her high-maintenance ass would be the perfect diversion from my thoughts.

It was only noon and Tasha had called four times already. I ignored the first three but picked up on the fourth.

"Yes," I snapped.

"Let me explain, Cass!" she said urgently.

"Oh, my bad, I thought the first words out of your mouth would've been 'I'm sorry' or 'I know I'm a backstabbing ho'. You know, something like that?"

Mia was heading toward me in the kitchen, so I had to cut the verbal assault short.

"Look, I gotta go. Have a nice life!" I said before hanging up.

Explain? Explain what? *Puhleeze!*

"C'mon, baby. You want apple juice or milk?" I asked Mia.

"Milk, please," she said as she climbed up on the stool of our breakfast bar.

I sat beside her and we housed our grilled cheese sandwiches. It ignited a fire inside my stomach. Felt like I hadn't eaten in days. *Shit, I don't think I have,* I thought.

"Nap time," I announced after lunch.

"Aw, Mommy."

"Nap time," I repeated.

"OK, OK. Can you read me a story first?" she asked. "Please, please, please?"

"All right. Go pick out a book and get up in your bed and wait for me, OK?"

"OK," she replied, skipping away.

I rinsed off our dishes and threw them in the dishwasher. I was wiping down the breakfast bar when the phone rang again.

It was my doctor's office.

"Is Ms. Stone available?"

"Hi, Dr. Wruth, it's me," I answered.

"We just got the results of your biopsy back," she announced.

"Yes," I said, holding my breath.

"You tested positive for human papillomavirus.

You actually have the advanced stage, and there are some precancerous cells on your cervix."

"Are you telling me I have cervical cancer, Dr. Wruth?"

"No. If you don't get this taken care of, then maybe. But right now the cells are precancerous and there's a procedure that can get rid of them. It's called LEEP. It will only take about thirty minutes or so. I usually like to put my patients under a mild anesthesia. There's no need to go all the way under, just a twilight should do."

"What about recovery? Will I be in a lot of pain?"

"Not at all. I would say ninety-five percent of my patients experience mild cramping and maybe a little spotting. Ibuprofen should take care of it, though."

"So I need to tell my partner, right?"

"Yes, anyone you've had unprotected sex with, and even protected sex too, Cassie."

Protected too? Payton . . . I honestly didn't want to believe that whatever was happening to me was not that serious. But now I have to discuss this with Payton. Great.

"But if we used protection, then why would I need to tell him anything?" I whined, realizing how pitiful I must've sounded. I really didn't want to have to tell Payton this. The walls began closing in around me.

"Mommy, I'm still waiting," I heard Mia yell in the distance.

"The virus can be transmitted from genital contact, not necessarily penetration and the exchange of fluids. So just tell any-one you've been intimate with, just to be sure.

"We've scheduled your LEEP for next Wednesday at six-thirty A.M. at the Tully Health Center. Do you know where that is?"

"Uh, yes, on Strawberry Hill, right?"

"Yes. Nothing to eat or drink after midnight Tuesday. You'll need someone to drive you home afterwards, OK?"

"OK."

"And don't worry, the procedure is minimally invasive and very routine."

"OK, thank you."

I traipsed down my short hallway, where Mia was waiting impatiently in her room.

I read her the book—with no enthusiasm in my voice. Just droned along reading the words. Soon enough she was asleep.

And I had two calls to make. Two very hard calls to make.

As I picked up the phone, though, it began ringing. The number showed private on my caller ID.

"Hello," I answered with attitude. I hated when people blocked their number.

"Yeah, uh, Cassie, you're not getting the message. How clear do you need me to send it? Stay the fuck away from my man, bitch."

"Who is this?" I yelled. I was too pissed to be scared this time.

"I'm your worst fucking nightmare! Stay away from Payton. Understand?" she screamed before hanging up.

Payton?

Chapter 25

Payton

Alana was always early to rise. If she was in a good mood, I'd see her most mornings before leaving for work. If she was in a bad mood, then she'd stay holed up in her room, listening to Amy Winehouse or John Legend. Recalling the meltdown she'd had the night before, I was surprised to see her downstairs eating a bowl of cereal.

"Good morning, Daddy," she said with a sweet voice.

"Hey, Sugar," I replied. "You feeling OK today?"

"Yeah, I am. You got in pretty late last night, mister. I'm sure you're feeling OK," she teased.

I just laughed off her suggestion. Then I had a flashback of Cassie's beautiful body riding on top of mine. Her gushy stuff on my face.

"Were you with that Cassie woman again? Tasha told me that you were all up on her that night you went out."

"And if I was?" I asked, wondering why she was getting all up in my business.

"Then I'd say you were stupid for just getting out of a relationship and now all up on another woman so soon."

"I know, Alana. Believe me, I've been around long enough to know better."

"Damn it!" she screamed. "Then why are you being so stupid?" she hollered. "Daddy, you deserve so much better. Take your time. Haven't you met any nice girls online yet?"

Her swinging moods were getting worse. I was starting to think that letting her read Keisha's letter had been a bad idea. It had sent her into a tizzy. Had a quick thought, I'd been forgetting to count her medication to make sure she wasn't missing any doses. 'Cause the way she was acting, I think she surely missed a dose or two.

"I'm grown. Don't worry about me and mines. What I need to be doing is meeting Parker."

Her face contorted, she got uncomfortable real quick. She scampered over to the sink, threw her bowl in and tried to rush away.

"Nope, you're not getting away with it that easy. I want to meet Parker, Alana. Soon. Friday night. We'll go to Eclisse. Friday at seven P.M."

"All right, fine," she said in defeat. "Friday at seven P.M."

"Sharp," I said with authority. Shoot, she must've lost her mind getting in my business. I had to take her down a level.

"Fine!" she yelled, now walking away.

As she turned around, I noticed a huge red mark on the side of her neck.

"Whoa, what the hell is that?" I yelled, pointing at the bruise that resembled a hickey on her neck.

She turned red and her mouth dropped open in surprise; she covered her neck with her hand. She was caught out.

"Huh?" she asked, eyes darting around the room.

"Huh, hell! If you can 'huh,' you can hear, damn it. Who put that hickey on your neck?"

My head was spinning. I wanted to choke her out for that tacky shit.

She looked around on the floor for her answer. Finally she responded with a whisper, "Parker."

"C'mon, Sugar. You're smarter than that. That's not cute. Don't ever let no man put his mark on you like that."

"I'm not a little girl anymore, Daddy. You can't think that I'm not going to be doing things."

"What the hell you mean, 'doing things'?"

I walked closer to her. Right in her face. She backed up a step. I stepped forward again.

I asked, "Are you having sex?"

Her eyes filled up with tears and she twitched violently. "Why would you ask me something like that?" she screamed.

I never got an answer, though. She stormed up the stairs, crying, and slammed her bedroom door behind her.

The subject seemed to upset her so badly that I decided to leave it alone. For now.

I got dressed and headed to work, despite the rocky start to my day. The thought that my little girl was possibly having sex was enough stress to have me seeking therapy.

The day dragged on as I pondered Alana and Parker having sex, plus I knew that I had the meeting with Keisha that night. I would put on my "I don't give a fuck" face, sign the papers and walk away. We had nothing to talk about.

Things went a little bit differently, though, when we met. Just a little. I worked a little late. Caught up on some filing and started preparing the monthly newsletter to pass the time. Left at 5:15 P.M. and was at Dunkin' Donuts right on time.

She was punctual as well. I ordered a black coffee with three sugars and took a seat facing the entrance. When she began approaching me, I was in shock. Same height. Same sandy brown hair, kissed with highlights of blond. But a whole different Keisha.

She looked like she weighed 250, a far cry from the petite one-thirty she was when we were together. Her cheeks looked like she was hiding acorns in them. Her once- expressive amber eyes had turned into tight slits, surrounded by gray circles. Lips once pink and soft were brown and looked like sandpaper—even through the thick layer of lip gloss she had caked on.

She strutted over and sat in the chair parallel from me.

Till death do us part.

"Payton," she greeted, very professionally.

"Keisha," I returned, just as cold.

"You look good," she said, with a lingering eye.

"Thank you," I responded, unable to return the compliment. And unwilling to fake it just to be polite. Not for her, she didn't deserve it.

"So here are the papers," she said, getting down to business. She kept nervously peering out the window.

I could see that her fiancé and children were impatiently waiting in the car for her.

"And here's a pen," she added, passing me the pen.

Scanning through the document, I didn't recognize most of the legalese. Irreconcilable differences. Agreed. Then five alarms went off in my head when I saw the box for joint custody of Alana Madison Johnson.

"Johnson? So you don't even know that I adopted her and changed her name to Harris? You don't even know her name and you want joint custody? No, I'm not signing this shit!"

I slammed the paper on the table and slid them back across the table to her.

"Do we have to take this to court then, Payton? Do I need to remind you that mothers rarely lose in custody battles? That my fiancé makes good money and we have a nice house."

"She doesn't want to see you, Keisha. You've

caused enough problems in her life. Why don't you just leave her alone?"

"You want to play hardball, Payton. Then I want full custody. She has no choice but to see me. I am her mother."

"She'll be eighteen in a year. You sound ridiculous. Custody. What, for a year? She's going to college in a few weeks. You're not making any sense."

"I just want to see my daughter and I don't know any better way to do it!" she yelled. Thick black makeup marched down her cheeks, making her look deranged. "I fucked up, P. I know that. But I'm a human being and I just want to see my daughter. I gave birth to her."

"I'm not signing those papers. Take me to court."

She stood up, breathing so heavy and crying so hard that I thought she might pass out. Her fiancé could pick up the pieces to her broken heart. The only person's heart I was concerned with was Alana's. Custody, ha!

I sat there arrogantly; my arms defiantly folded across my chest. She ran out of Dunkin' Donuts as fast as her short, thick legs would carry her. I watched through the window as she hopped in the car and sped off.

I guzzled the rest of my lukewarm coffee and headed to my car. I'll be damned if the back window wasn't smashed in.

"What the fuck!" I yelled, running toward my car.

Inside I saw a brick with a piece of paper attached by a rubber band. Someone must've seen something.

"Sir, sir!" I said, yelling to the Hispanic man selling newspapers. "Did you see who did this?"

He shook his head.

I reached in from the front seat and grabbed the brick. Ripped off the rubber band and unfolded the letter.

If I can't have you, then no one can!

I let the letter drop into my lap and immediately pulled out my phone and dialed Summer. She was getting out of hand.

Of course she didn't answer but I let her have it on voice mail, advising her that if she continued with her shenanigans, I would call the police. I wanted to tell her that I was going to choke her to death when I saw her again, but I didn't want to leave any evidence. I was surely going to *kill* her!

Chapter 26

Cassie

By the end of the week, I felt confident that Mia was ready to go back to camp. Plus. she was begging me to go back, insisting she was fine. And I had much business to handle, so I dropped her off and told the camp senior counselor to keep a close eye on her and call me if she was the slightest bit concerned about Mia.

The threatening call I received the day before had me a little shook-up. I figured it must've been Payton's ex-girlfriend that he'd told me about. Payton would surely have to get this chick in check, because I had a daughter at home and I didn't need that drama.

After the call I made sure all the locks on the door were secured and peered out the window to make sure she wasn't stalking me. Like a mother in the wild, I went into protective mode and lay on Mia's floor as she slept. I ended up napping too. When I woke up, I didn't have the energy or courage to make the calls to Brice and Payton. It would have to wait until the next day.

The next day I decided to make the easiest call first: Brice. I didn't give a damn about him after finding out about him and Tasha. I silently reveled in the possibility of him having passed it on to Tasha as well. The thought quickly dissipated when I realized that she could've passed it to *me*.

Pissed, I dialed his cell phone number.

He answered, "I'm on my way to the airport. I don't have time for this now."

"Oh, you think I'm calling to beef with you about Tasha? No, honey, I'm over that," I lied, trying to save face. "I'm actually calling for something kind of serious."

"Talk fast," he sighed, sounding bored.

"Look," I shot, tired of his front, "I tested positive for HPV, the strain that causes cervical cancer, so you'll need to get treated so you don't pass it around."

I started to hang up, afraid of how he might react.

"What is HPV, Cassie?" he asked, sounding less than enthused.

"It's a very common STD. You probably have no symptoms and neither did I. I'm going to get the cancerous cells removed, and I hope you're smart enough to seek treatment as well."

"You gave me some shit, Cassie? What, so you was fucking me and that Payton cat at the same time, huh?" he yelled, now completely interested in what I was talking about.

"Don't you dare! Don't you dare try to turn this on me. Isn't that just like a coward, trying to shift the focus on me because your ass is trifling. *You* betrayed *me*, Brice. I will never forget that. Ever! You keep disrespecting me and watch what happens!" I threatened.

"What you gonna keep me from seeing my daughter?"

"You really don't know me at all, do you? No. I would never do that. Only for Mia's sake, though. Don't you worry, but I'll think of something. Respect me. I deserve better than that."

Then I really did hang up, my job was done. He knew about my status. I didn't care if he kept HPV so long that his dick fell off.

In a tizzy I called Payton.

He answered, "Hey, beautiful." There was no smile in his voice, though.

"Hey, uh, Payton. It's, uh, Cassie. Um, can we meet up somewhere? I really need to talk to you. In person. Soon."

I knew if I didn't tell him soon, I'd never muster up enough courage to tell him again. All the adrenaline running through my body from the call with Brice filled me with false confidence.

"Wanna come by the camp? We can talk privately in my office. Is everything OK? You don't sound too tough," he noticed.

"Actually, no. No, everything's not OK. Everything's a disaster!" I broke down crying. I was tired of keeping things from him. Hiding my emotions as not to scare him away. Tired of pretending so I didn't rustle his feathers. Who the hell was he that I felt I had to front? Furthermore, I just really, really needed someone to talk to. Needed to vent and cry and get a lot off my chest.

"Cassie, don't cry. You know where Horizons camp is, right? Come now, OK? I've been wanting to talk to you too."

I pulled up to the camp ten minutes later. I saw Payton waiting outside the gym door. He flagged me over.

I walked cautiously. I'd come down off my false-confidence high and now was feeling extremely vulnerable and apprehensive. The conversation that we were about to have was going to be a defining moment in our relationship. Not that we had much of a relationship to speak of, but still.

He reached out to embrace me as soon as I was close enough. His hug sent shivers through my body. I rested my head on Payton's firm chest and it felt right. He rubbed his hand through my hair.

"C'mon, let's get outta this sun," he suggested.

My knees wobbled as I followed Payton into his air-conditioned office in the back of the gym. I'd seen the kids outside playing kickball on the baseball diamond, so I knew we'd have privacy for a while.

"Sit down." He offered the cushion seat to me while he took a seat on the wooden fold-up chair directly across from me.

"I have HPV," I blurted out before I even knew

it. *What the hell is wrong with you,* I thought, immediately feeling ashamed. My nerves had gotten
the best of me. "I'm sorry, I didn't know until
yesterday. I contracted it from Brice."

"You know what's funny?" he began.

Funny, what the heck was wrong with this dude?

"When me and Summer first started dating,
she had the same problem from her previous relationship. So I got tested and treated about five
months ago for it. Don't worry. I know all about
it. I'll just go get checked out again to make sure
I'm straight."

"Are you serious?" I asked, feeling measurably
better already, and letting out a nervous laugh.

Telling Payton I could've possibly given him
an STD was one of the hardest things I ever had
to do. But it was over! Whew.

Before he could answer, I said, "Speaking of
Summer . . . I think she left me a threatening
note and called my house yesterday telling me to
stay away from you."

"You've gotta be kidding me!" he screamed,
catapulting out of his chair.

With his palms on the top of his head, he
yelled, "I can't believe this shit! I told you she's
making this breakup harder than it needs to be."

"How does she even know about me? She
knows me by name, Payt."

"I have no idea! She has really crossed the
fucking line this time. I promise you, I'll take
care of it."

He couldn't be still. He paced quickly back and forth.

"I'm sorry," he said. "I'll take care of this," he told me again.

"Payt, sit down. I'm not scared of her like that. Mia's my concern. Summer knows my name and has my number, so she probably knows where I live."

He sat back down.

"And I just wanted to tell you a couple more things while we're sharing," I said.

Through tears I told him about Mia's sickle-cell disease. He shared Alana's manic depression with me. Our lives seemed parallel, the more we opened up to each other.

It felt great talking to Payton about my baggage. I was pleasantly surprised that he let me in and didn't shut down on me. Not once. Every question I asked about Alana, he answered. Just as every question he asked about Mia, I answered.

It was almost noon, so Payton ordered us some pizza and salad to be delivered for lunch.

"Stay and have lunch with me?"

"Sure. I have one more bomb to drop, and then I'm done."

He smiled. "Drop the bomb, baby."

I told him about Tasha and Brice, and his jaw hit the floor. I told him that I didn't know if I'd ever forgive Tasha or Brice.

"I don't blame you. If Damon was to do that to me, we'd have to knuckle up."

I excused myself to the bathroom. I gathered

myself while I was in there, and when I came back, he was looking down at his hands. His leg was shaking.

"Can I drop a bomb on you now?" he asked, unsure.

"Of course," I said, taken back by his openness.

"I am still legally married to Alana's mother."

Married! Now it was my jaw gathering dust from the floor. He went on to explain the circumstances, and I'll be damned if I didn't start crying again.

"So what happened to her that night? The night she left you guys?"

"I still don't know."

"You should ask her!" I insisted.

"Well, she and I aren't really on the same page right now. I went to sign the divorce papers yesterday, and for some reason this psycho is trying to get partial custody of Alana. She's seventeen!"

"Are you serious? In a year Alana will legally be an adult. What's her point?"

"Exactly. She's just being selfish. She wants to be able to see Alana, but Alana's not having it."

When we got all the heavy topics out of the way, we sat on the floor of his office eating pizza, talking and laughing like old friends. I hadn't felt so good . . . since the last time he and I were together.

Chapter 27

Payton

I hadn't seen Damon in a few days. His schedule as a fireman kept him working for days at a time. But his series of twenty-four-hour shifts for the week had ended, so we met up at Café Moja for some Caribbean food for dinner.

I arrived first, as always; so before I went inside I called Summer for the eightieth time that day. She finally answered.

"And what is the reason for your incessant calling?" she answered.

"Don't you play stupid, Summer. Look, if you don't stop fucking with me, I'm going to call the cops on your deranged ass. I should take you to small-claims court and make you pay for the vandalism you've done to my car too. And what's the deal with you messing with Cassie? She ain't never did nothing to you!"

"I'm not fighting with you anymore, Payton. I'm just not. I have no idea what the hell you are talking about. And who's Cassie? Huh? Is that the bitch you kicked me to the curb for?"

"So you're going to continue playing stupid? It ends here, Summer. No more threats to me or Cassie. You hear?"

Summer roared with laughter. The maniacal noise pierced through the phone and stung my ear.

"Payton, please. You're feeling yourself. I am over you! Been over you. Call the cops. Play detective. Good luck. 'Cause it ain't me, nigga!"

She knew I hated *that* word more than anything. Use "punk", "sissie", "asshole." But *that* word was never OK. Particularly when meant to be an insult. My hesitance let her know that I was about to explode. Before I could explode, she'd hung up. The menacing laugh trailing off and then coming to an abrupt halt.

The phone rang right back. It was Keisha.

"You revised those papers yet?" I answered before she could begin.

"No—"

"Then we don't have nothing to talk about," I said before hanging up and powering my phone off.

The vein in my forehead pulsated. Hot blood ran through my veins. My nose flared. Fists clenched.

Damon walked up just in the nick of time. Literally, my head was about to explode.

"'Sup, dog?" he said, giving me a pound. We reached in for half a hug.

"Man, listen," I said, shaking my head. "I gotta

catch you up on everything. My world is upside down."

We sat at the bar and I ordered the jerk shrimp. Damon, the stewed chicken.

It was draining to fill him in on the letter, Alana's mood swings, Summer's psycho ass and Keisha's selfish ass. But I guess there is something to be said about getting things off your chest. I didn't do it often, but I did feel a little lighter after telling him everything.

"And what's up with you and Tasha?" I asked after I finished my rampage.

I hoped nothing, because she was sharing dicks like music downloads.

"Na, that ain't nothing. Not the type of chick I'd take it any further with, you know what I mean? I mean, she's cool and all, but she just doesn't have the 'it' factor to make me stay around, ya know?"

I told him about Tasha sleeping with Brice.

"That's crazy!" he yelled.

"I know. Damn shame. Cassie's her homegirl."

"Well, what's the first two letters in homegirl? *Ho!* Women gotta watch their closest friends more than anyone."

"Preach!"

"Oh, shit! I forgot to tell you. I saw Summer the other day. Looked like a disaster area. Her hair was short and matted to her head. Her clothes were baggy and faded. I think she's losing weight over you, man. The bags under her eyes were swollen and dark. I mean, she just looked a mess."

"For real? Damn."

For a moment—for a *moment*—I felt bad for her again. Only because I would never want anyone that distraught because of me. But the moment of sympathy passed like a summer rainstorm.

"Oh, yeah, and next Saturday is our annual father-daughter cookout at the firehouse. Tell Alana I said this year is our year to win first place in something! *Something. Anything.* Last year we lost the three-legged race by this much," he explained, pinching his pointer and thumb together to show me.

Damon, of course, didn't have a daughter of his own, so Alana always went to his annual cookout and they'd have the best time together. Damon's nothing more than a big kid.

"I'll tell her, but with the way she's been acting lately, it's hit-or-miss with her nowadays."

"Oh, please. I'm her fun daddy. She'd never turn me down," he boasted.

"Yeah you're fun because you don't have to worry about paying her cell phone bill, keeping a roof over her head, buying her Seven jeans and keeping the electricity on."

"Precisely!" he agreed as we exploded in laughter.

But Damon wasn't a deadbeat godfather. Not at all. Along the way he'd spent a lot of time with Alana and always bought her a few things for back-to-school, her birthday and Christmas. And since I still had to pay out of pocket for Alana's room and board at NYU, he offered to pay 25 percent of the costs and buy her books.

"It's dangerous out here with no education," he'd explained to me back when I found out the huge amount of money I'd still have to pony up. "We're going to make sure nothing gets in the way of her finishing school. Not money—nothing!"

We finished up our dinner and were about to go our separate ways when I had the urge to tell him about my growing feelings for Cassie, but then thought wiser of it. He'd just tease me and make me feel like a punk about it, so I kept it to myself. Furthermore, I still had several weeks before Alana went to college, so I didn't want to get serious about Cassie just yet.

I got home before 8:00 P.M. and Alana was sprawled across the couch watching TV.

"Hey, baby, I brought you some jerk shrimp home for dinner," I announced.

"Hey, Daddy, thanks. I just had some cereal, but I'll eat it later," she responded, not taking her eyes off the screen.

I walked past her into the kitchen and put the container of food in the fridge.

"How you feeling today?" I asked her, returning to the living room.

"All right. Why?"

"Why? I gotta have a reason? Just making conversation."

"Umph," she responded. "You been on SexyCTSingles.com yet?"

"Haven't checked it lately, but I went on once or twice."

"Umph. OK then. I hope Ms. Right hasn't come along while you've been sniffing around in a mutt's yard."

I wanted to put her in her place. Wanted to check her. I really did. But I was tired of all the conflict. I just wanted everything back to how it was before Summer. I wanted my Sugar back.

"I will log on tonight, OK, Sugar?"

She looked at me for the first time that evening. "OK, can you go get me my shrimp now?"

Her moods were swinging so fast, I couldn't keep up anymore. I retrieved her meal from the fridge and handed it to her.

"I'm going to take a shower and then log right on. OK, Ms. Matchmaker?"

"OK," she giggled.

As I headed upstairs, I seized the opportunity to sneak into Alana's room and check her medicine. I cursed myself for not keeping count lately, but it appeared that everything was in order. The bottle was half empty.

After I showered, I did as promised and logged on to the dating Web site. There were six messages waiting for me—three from EvenSweeter. The first one I deleted right away without bothering to read the note. Her screen name was NaughtyLadyXXX. No thanks. Maybe ten years ago though. PhenomenalWoman left a note asking me what some of my hobbies were and if I belonged to a fraternity. I didn't answer her right away or go to her profile page to see what she looked like either. I was anxious to get to EvenSweeter's notes, since there were three of them and we'd already spoken before. I vividly remembered the shot of her legs from her profile.

Before checking her notes, I went to her profile page to see if she'd updated her picture—she had. It was a profile shot of her light-and-sweet coffee midsection. Her jeans tight, shirt short, exposing her flat stomach free of stretch marks. Intrigued, I went back to read her notes.

Hello. I've been waiting for you to write me. Playing hard to get?

The second note, sent a day later, read: I can't say that I enjoy being ignored by you. ☹

The third, sent just a few minutes ago: I missed you. Missed you so much I followed you today. LOL. Remember that line from the Orange Juice Jones song? LMAO. But I really did follow you today. Wanted to see who was occupying all the time you weren't using on getting to know me! But I saw that you were just with your friend from the picture on your profile. I love Caribbean food too, especially jerk shrimp. Now will you write me back?!?!?

My first instinct was to quickly turn to look behind me, like I expected someone to be there holding a butcher knife over my head. Of course there was no one there.

"I knew I shouldn't have done this on-line

dating thing!" I yelled, quickly shutting the computer down.

My palms were moist as I wrung them together. The air from the ceiling fan kept hitting the beads of sweat forming on the back of my neck, causing me to feel a little tickle that made me jump.

EvenSweeter? Who the hell can she be?

Couldn't be Summer, 'cause she didn't even know how to send a damn text message. Plus, the pictures on the online profile definitely weren't her. The pictures could be fake, though, I reasoned. No, that's not her style. Must be someone else. But who?

Chapter 28

Cassie

"Every time I see you,
You pretend like you don't see me.
I know you feel me,
Stop being shy
You know that I'm that guy.
Why you playin' games with me girl?"

I was in my car on the way to the grocery store listening to WBLS when the song came on. I pulled over my car so fast that the tires screeched and I came to a hard stop.

The voice was familiar. The song was too—I wrote it! The words were floating over a bass heavy-down-south kind of beat. Lil Wayne popped on midway through the song and ripped it, rapping about how the shy girl needs to come out of her shell.

"That was newcomer Brice Morgan with 'Shy Girl,' The song is bananas! Remember you heard it here first, because this song is about to burn up the charts. Ladies, he'll be in the studio with

me in less than an hour, so make sure you call up
and show this brother some love. I hear he's easy
on the eyes too, ladies!"

Was I losing my memory? Because I clearly
didn't remember signing anything to release the
rights to my song.

My cell phone rang. I didn't even bother looking to see who it was. Tasha was squealing on the
other line.

"He published your song!" she screamed.
"That's your song, Cassie!"

For a brief moment I pushed our tiff aside—
this new development took precedence! She was
at work, so she must've been streaming the station from their Web site.

"I know. I know!"

"Now, I know he doesn't have your permission
to use that song. You can sue him, Cassie!"

"My song didn't have Lil Wayne and the hot
beat behind it, though. Damn!"

As mad as I was about him stealing my lyrics—
the song was fire! I loved it!

"Yeah, I don't like the way! The song is hot!"

"Me neither!" I screamed into the phone. "I
gotta talk to a lawyer. I don't know what to do!"

Everything I said was in a high-pitch shrill. My
hands immediately started to sweat. My eyes
darted from side to side like a crack fiend. I
tapped my hands against the steering wheel.
Tasha's mouth was going a mile a minute and I
couldn't understand half of what she was saying
because she was screaming too.

"Cassie! Cassie? You listening to me," she screamed.

I snapped outta my thoughts.

"Yeah. I'm—I'm listening."

"Can you come by my office? We really need to talk. I have to explain everything to you. We gotta make this right. I've been miserable without you!"

"OK, OK. What time?"

"Now! You know I do's what I want to around here. I wish they would say something to me. We can go in the conference room and order some lunch and talk."

I didn't want to be upset with Tasha anymore. Wanted to talk things through. Wanted an explanation. Deserved an explanation. Hoped it would be a good one too. If not, then it would be hard to get past the fact that she slept with Brice.

Didn't take long to get up High Ridge Road to her job at Xerox. The receptionist announced my arrival and Tasha came out to meet me.

There was an awkward moment. An unpleasant realization that we'd shared the same man filled the air and choked me.

Tasha hugged me and I wanted to vomit. Did I not know the two people that I considered closest to me over the past decade at all? He stole my song. She stole my man . . . if only for one night. Or day. Or whenever. Ugh. The vomit resurfaced in my throat. I forced it down with a hard swallow.

"C'mon, the conference room is over here," she directed.

She already ordered some J. Lo rolls and chicken Teriyaki from Kam Pei. The smell teased my empty stomach.

We sat across from each other like colleagues, not sisters.

"So?" I asked, looking for my explanation right away.

I grabbed a J. Lo roll and spread some wasabi and soy sauce over it. From the first bite, it felt like an orgy in my mouth.

Tasha dug right into the chicken and started explaining.

"It was a long, long time ago, Cassie. Before you even had Mia. Back in the Indigo days—"

"As many women as he cheated on me with! You mean to tell me you were one of them hos?" I interrupted, all the anger immediately resurfacing.

She ignored my insult and continued.

"It was one night when you were in Boston visiting your grandfather. We went to Apples, like we always did every Friday night after rehearsal. We smoked a little chief before we got there. Then I had about four margaritas."

"Blaming it on the liquor, huh? That's so whack."

Again she ignored my baiting.

"Cassie, he took advantage of me!" she said, slamming her fist on the table. "That's why we started fighting all the time. I didn't want to have sex with him. I told him no, over and over again. But I was so drunk that I couldn't drive home. I guess my mistake was not calling a cab. I should've never let him take me home!

"We got to my house and he undressed me and put me in the bed. I must've blacked out or something, because next thing I knew, he was inside me. The next moments that passed are spotty. I remember opening my eyes and telling him to get the fuck off me. Then I remember opening my eyes again and trying to spit on him. He put his hand over my mouth, and then I blacked out again.

"When I woke up the next morning, he was sleeping beside me naked."

I couldn't swallow everything she was telling me. I started crying. She started crying.

"I wailed on his ass that morning. Told him to get the fuck out of my house. Remember those scratches he couldn't explain? You thought they were from wild sex with a groupie. They were from me. I was trying to kill that man. Told him that I was going to tell you as soon as you got back from Boston. But that's when he told me that you guys had just found out you were pregnant. 'You'd be ruining a family, not just a relationship now,' he told me.

"So I decided not to say anything, but that's why I have so much hatred against him. He's trifling!"

"He raped you, Tasha. You should've told me."

"No, it wasn't rape. He was just being a cave-man and took advantage of me."

"He raped you!" I screamed, disgusted that I bore his child.

"Shhh," she told me, putting her index finger up to her lips. I'd forgotten we were at her job. "I didn't want to be the one to break up the family. But as soon as I saw you were serious about leaving his ass alone, I wanted to tell you. I went to Brice and suggested that we tell you together. He refused. I told him that if he wouldn't tell me with you, that I was going to tell you anyway. Then he threatened to flip the story around and make me look like I seduced him. Like *I* seduced him! Yeah, right. He's not even my type like that."

"So that's why you were at his house that day?"

"Yes. I didn't know you'd be there, though, but when I saw your car there, I thought, even better! I was going to talk to him face-to-face because he'd been ignoring my phone calls all week."

"Damn," I responded.

"Look, it's Friday. I'ma go tell my boss I'm leaving early."

The food was picked over and half eaten. I'd long since lost my appetite halfway through her sick story.

Tasha stood up and came around the table to hug me. We embraced and rocked each other back and forth.

"You still my sister?" she asked.

"You still mine? I called you a ho."

"You know it! Hey, let's have a sleepover at my house tonight? Get some movies and popcorn for the girls, and me and you can do some catching up. I missed you!"

"And I missed you like Salt misses Pepa."

Chapter 29

Payton

Alana's manic phases? She's over-the-top happy and seems like she has no memory of anything bad ever happening. She's all smiles and jokes, like she's possessed by a naïve six-year-old.

When I entered the house and heard a chorus of two jovial female voices coming from the kitchen, I figured that Missy was over again. Alana's voice carried the innocent bubbliness that I'd learned to associate with her manic personality. I exhaled heavily, thankful that she was in a happy mood at least.

I realized after kicking off my shoes at the door that the voice didn't belong to Missy, and it damn sure sounded too familiar. *No way*, I thought.

I rounded the corner, and no, my ears weren't deceiving me—Keisha was sitting at my kitchen table with Alana.

Careful not to upset Alana, I calmly asked Keisha what she was doing here.

"Came by to see my daughter. I have rights,

Payton. I just . . . I just couldn't go without seeing her." She smiled.

"Daddy, can you believe it? She said she's loved me all along?"

I was in a parallel universe battling with myself about kicking Keisha's ass out. She wouldn't be around to pick up the pieces of Alana's broken heart after today's visit.

"Can I talk to you outside, Keisha?"

She looked up at me like she didn't plan on budging.

"Now," I said with conviction. "Alana, I'll only be a minute."

"OK," she replied, "I have some leftover chicken from last night in the oven for lunch. It's almost done."

Keisha followed me out to the porch and plopped her sloppy body on the bench.

"You can't keep me from seeing my daughter. I love her too, Payton."

"Keisha, what you don't understand is that she's not well. I wish you would've listened to me and respected my wishes."

"What do you mean she's not well? She looks great. Payton, she really is so beautiful. Doesn't she look just like I did back in the day?"

Even though Keisha was in the wrong for showing up unannounced, she was genuinely ecstatic to see Alana. I was torn, but I just knew this couldn't be good for Alana.

"She tells me that she's going to NYU in a few

weeks. Can you believe it?" Keisha gushed like she had something to be proud of.

"Keisha, it's not good that you showed up like this. She doesn't handle change well. I mean, when I told her that you wanted to see herm she was very adamant about *not* seeing you. I can't even believe she's so happy.

"She—she was diagnosed with bipolar disorder a few years ago. Right now—the person you see in there is not the real her. She's manic right now. Which means she's on this super high, but, Keisha, when she comes down, she's going to come down hard. She's taking medicine to stabilize it, but she just started this new prescription, so I don't think she's adjusted fully to it yet."

"Bipolar disorder? You let some doctor tell you that our daughter has a mental illness? She just misses her mother, that's all. Any little girl raised without her mother around will go through things."

"No! You don't live with her, and you haven't seen her go through these high highs and low lows. It's very real, Keisha. She's ill."

"That's the problem with today's society. All they want to do is fill people up with drugs, instead of getting them the nurturing they need. Now, all of a sudden a badass kid has ADHD. What happened to just being a badass? Now a teenager going through regular teenage shit that we all went through is suffering from depression or bipolar disorder. Being a teenage girl is all about being a raging bitch one day and the picture of sweetness the next."

"No, Keisha, the problem with us—black folks—is that we always think we're supposed to hold the world on our shoulders. Since we endured slavery and segregation, we should be able to handle a little stress, like depression, without proper help. Wake up! This is real. She has a chemical imbalance and she needs real help!"

The rims of Keisha's eyes were suddenly red and tears began flowing down her face.

"Keisha, I tried my best to give her a great childhood. I did my best. It's just one of those things that can't be helped."

"It's my fault, P. If I would've never left, she'd be OK."

As much as I would love for her selfish ass to carry that guilt, I couldn't let her, because it was just untrue.

"It's no one's fault. That's what I'm trying to tell you."

"Can I stay? Please?" she begged. "I want to try to make things right. I have seventeen years to make up to her. Can't you just give me a few more hours?"

"Whatever you do, don't bring up her mental health. She might get defensive and fall into her depressive state. She's liable to pick up a knife and try to stab you."

Keisha wiped her eyes as she waddled and jiggled back into the house.

The next few hours were grueling for me. I took my plate upstairs to my room after Alana finished lunch and I let the girls have their time alone. The whole time I was on pins and needles, hoping the visit wouldn't turn ugly. But everything worked out fine. It was an uneventful evening.

Alana yelled up, "Daddy, Keisha's leaving now. Come say good-bye!"

I walked Keisha to her car and in the most polite way possible told her to never show up unannounced again. Giving her my number, I said, "Call first next time."

"I will, and I'm sorry. I just knew that if I didn't do this, you would've never let me see her. She said she wants to come to Brooklyn to see her sisters and brothers. What do you think?"

"We'll just take it one day at a time, OK?"

I turned and walked away from her, anxious to see how Alana was holding up.

"So what do you think?" I asked her. Her back was to me as she washed the dishes.

She turned around, allowing her wet hands to drip water on the floor.

"What do I think?" she whispered. I noted her high-octave manic voice was gone. "I think she better not ever come here again! How dare she? And how dare you let her come here? I hate you and I hate her! Nobody really cares about me. You can stop pretending now. I'm a big girl!"

I felt like running out the front door, screaming. I knew it was coming, she was not ready to see her mother. Slowly I approached her and reached out to give her a hug. I had no idea what to say. I knew she didn't mean half of what she'd said, and the visit had gone well. Her body and mind just didn't know how to process this wave of emotions.

"Don't touch me!" she screamed before she hit the floor.

This was the craziest shit I'd ever seen. She started kicking and screaming like a two-year-old throwing a temper tantrum, screaming "Don't touch me," over and over again.

I backed away with caution and said, "I'm not. I won't touch you. Calm down."

But I had to get her out of the kitchen with all the glass and knives that she could hurt herself with. I didn't know what to do next.

Just then she sprang to her feet and grabbed the steak knife from the counter and haphazardly threw it toward me.

I sidestepped to avoid getting hit and lunged toward her, grabbing her and hoisting her over my shoulder. Alana's legs and arms flailed wildly as I struggled to carry her up the stairs. By the time we reached the top, she'd seem to have calmed down a bit. No longer screaming and kicking, she just sobbed loudly.

I placed her down carefully, and she stood, frozen in front of me, leering at me with fear-glazed eyes.

"I'm so sorry I threw the knife at you. I wasn't trying to hurt you," she whispered. "I don't hate you. I love you. I love you so much," she said as she buried her head into my chest and cried some more. "But I hate her. I do."

"Well, I would've gotten rid of her right away. Why didn't you tell me that you didn't want her here? You seemed so happy to finally meet her."

"I don't know what was wrong with me. I didn't want to be happy, but for some reason I couldn't help it," she cried. "Can we just forget what happened today? I'm so sorry."

"Forgotten," I promised her.

"I'm going to bed now for a little nap."

She headed toward her room and closed the door softly.

I stood in the middle of the hallway, spent from the day's developments. Feeling like I didn't know how much more of her illness I could take alone. I longed for a wife to be around to help her. How would she ever be able to go away to college with her illness still not under control?

Chapter 30

Cassie

I'd thought about the conversation Tasha and I had that afternoon. Something in me didn't trust her excuse about not wanting to break up our happy home. Something in me told me that she said what she needed to say in order to keep our friendship together. I mean, at the time it felt good to get the answers I've been looking for, and I took what she said at face value. Brice had raped her and taken advantage of her. But too many pieces just didn't make sense. The Tasha that I knew never held her tongue. *Not ever.*

Although I knew we'd get through this ordeal, I didn't feel like jumping headfirst back into our friendship. I canceled the sleepover. Wanted to be alone with Mia that night. Needed to speak with Brice and get his side of the story. But that bastard stole my song and I just couldn't imagine having a civilized conversation with him anytime soon.

Desperately needing to escape my reality, I decided to get a professional massage and do some self-reflection. Here I was, a child raised in a two-parent home, filled with love and laughter—provided every opportunity to make a great life for myself—what happened?

I entered the spa and announced that I didn't have an appointment but would wait for the next available masseuse. I was shown to the back, where they gave me a robe, slippers and showed me to the mineral pool, where I could relax until it was my turn.

The peaceful ambience made me relax immediately. The bubbling pool purred softly and the low lighting made me feel a bit sleepy. I was alone in this little oasis and it was just what I needed.

About ten minutes later I was called into a stately tan room with the strong aroma of vanilla and lavender wafting through the air. My masseur was a petite nondescript white man with muscular arms and a gentle disposition. He turned on some classical music which was barely audible, and I lay down on the table. He instructed me to take five deep breaths and then he would begin.

His buttery soft hands began caressing my body, and my thoughts drifted back to my so-called life.

How was it that I'd become such a bad judge in character? I always seemed to be the person getting hurt and never the person doing the hurting. I needed to resolve not to be so nice anymore. Nice girls always finish last. Tasha and Brice had slept together. Do I not have anyone in my life that's loyal?

How was it that I was a receptionist making just

enough money for me and my daughter to survive off? How did I allow a man to come between me and my dreams? I let Brice pursue his dreams, while my life became devoted to taking care of him and Mia.

Then there was Payton. Could I ever let another man around Mia? I wondered if he wanted more kids one day. Did I even want more kids? I guess I couldn't picture myself with more kids. I could never imagine loving another human being as much as I love my Mia.

I also had anxiety hanging over my head about undergoing the LEEP, and cervical cancer was no joke. So I'd heard anyway.

My mind became flooded with too many thoughts to count. I thought of one thing and something came right behind it. So much so, I wasn't able to enjoy my massage. And that was not what I'd come for. I let my mind go blank and then thought about good things. Like taking Mia to the beach and making sundaes with all types of crazy toppings.

Soon I wasn't haunted by any thoughts at all. I was just able to enjoy the music and the pleasure of the massage.

I left forty-five minutes later, feeling like I had more questions than I had come in there with. At least I was relaxed, and I decided to leave some of the questions in that stately tan room, because there were no answers to them. Some things just were . . . and there's nothing I could do about it.

Chapter 31

Payton

I was more than ready to meet Parker. Because of yesterday's events, she just wanted to stay home. She told me she called Parker and rescheduled our dinner. We made plans to meet him at P.F. Chang's in Westchester at 7:00 P.M.

Alana came down the stairs, looking stunning. She wore a shimmery peach dress with thin straps and gold shoes. Around her neck she wore the gold cross I'd given her for Christmas.

"You look lovely, Sugar."

"Why, thank you. And you don't look too bad yourself."

I'd worn a suit. Tan, with a baby blue shirt underneath. We made a handsome pair that night with our matching pastel colors.

"You look nervous," I told her. She wouldn't make eye contact with me. "I'm not going to scare your little punk boyfriend away. I just want to meet him, that's all. We're going to have a good time tonight. I'll be on my best behavior."

"Promise, Daddy?"

"I promise," I said, putting up the Scout's honor hand.

We arrived at P.F. Chang's right on time.

"Do you want to wait out here for him or should we just take a seat?" I asked Alana.

"Let's just sit down," she suggested.

The restaurant was crowded and bustling with laughter and chatter. The hostess led us through the crowd to our booth in the back.

"Your server will be right with you. Enjoy your evening!" the petite Asian hostess told us before sauntering off.

There was something strange going on with Alana. I'd never seen her so nervous before. But it wasn't a regular nervous. She looked like a battered wife dreading her husband's return home after a long night of drinking. Her disposition made me hate the kid already. But I promised I'd behave myself. Damn it!

Trying to ease her mind, I told her about the psycho stalker on SexyCTSinlges.com. She offered a weak chuckle.

Thankfully, our server came to our table and offered us some drinks. I ordered a Hennessy and Coke; Alana wanted just a Coke.

"Are you still expecting one more?" she asked.

"Yes," I answered.

"What's wrong, Sugar?"

My heart was beginning to beat fast, hands getting shaky. I envisioned myself grabbing Parker by his scrawny neck and pulling him over the table. Whispering in his ear that I would kill him if he ever put a finger on my daughter. Then slamming his ass down in the seat and enjoying our meal.

"I'm fine," she said. "I just wanted him to make a good impression and he's already late."

"It's fine. We've only been here, like, five minutes. I'm sure he'll be here soon."

We ordered appetizers and waited until 8:45 P.M. before ordering our entrees without him. Alana poked her food around on her plate.

I offered, "He probably just got lost."

She added, "Yeah, and I left my cell phone at home so he can't even call me."

Any boy that didn't want to meet a girl's father meant he wasn't serious about her, or he had something to hide. He knew I'd see right through him. I didn't tell Alana that, though. I stuck with the lost theory. And that worked well for her as she stopped poking at her food and began eating it.

We quietly finished our meal. My heart was broken for her, and at that point I never wanted to meet Parker because I would not be able to hold my tongue about him standing her up. Standing *us* up.

"Well, we're all dressed up. Wanna go dancing with an old man?" I asked.

"Sure. But how will I get in? I'm not twenty-one."

"Don't worry. I know some people over at 'The Place.'"

"'The Place?' I heard it's so nice."

"Yeah, and it's still early, so it should be fairly empty. Let's go."

On the way to "The Place," Alana sullenly stared out the window.

"Sorry, Daddy. You must hate Parker now," she said.

"Well, he lost major points with me tonight. You deserve better than that. But let him know he's not off the hook. I still want to meet him. Next time we can just meet him at his house, so he can't possibly get lost."

She didn't laugh. Oh, well.

It was so early that no one was manning the door checking for ID, so we were able to walk right in. "The Place" was empty except for the staff and Otis. Otis was there rain or shine, noon or midnight. He was a player-player from way back and was my connection to allowing Alana in the establishment. Funny, because he didn't even work there. But since he was a permanent fixture, he had some major clout.

"Otis!" I yelled over the music.

Otis was always something else. High yellow with long, curly hair, which he kept parted on the side, and swept dramatically over the other side, he came barreling toward us. His money green silk shirt was perfectly complemented by his green gator shoes and mustard yellow slacks. His thick rope chain matched his gold belt and two gold front teeth.

"What's up, playboy?" I asked him after we gave each other a pound.

"Ain't nothing," he responded. His voice permanently hoarse from decades of cigarette smoking.

"You remember my daughter, Alana. Alana, this is Otis. You met him when you were a baby."

Alana reached out to shake his hand. He pulled her hand up to his greasy lips and kissed it.

For the first time in a long time, Alana exploded in laughter.

"See the effect I have on these girls. I'm trynna tell ya something, boy, if you ain't listening."

Huh? Otis was full of one-liners that never made any sense, but somehow you knew what he meant.

"Look, Otis, we don't plan to be in here long. She's only seventeen. You know me, I'm not trying to slip her a drink or nothing. I just want to show my daughter a good time, and then we're going to get out of here before the crowd starts pouring in, OK?"

"Boy, Otis run the show and ain't no show wit'out Otis. Pretty lady wanna come dance and no sin in that. Ain't nobody gon' say nothing to you," he explained with a defiant wave of his heavily ringed hand. "Look at you, as pretty as you wanna be," he told Alana with a wink. The he turned on his heels and glided away.

"He is crazy," Alana said. "I like him!"

I was happy that Otis lightened her mood. I sure couldn't have cheered her up as fast.

The DJ was playing a Prince mix ever since we'd walked in. "Erotic City" was on when Alana and I hit the dance floor.

"I don't know how to dance to this mess, Daddy." She was doing an awkward two-step. "This is way before my time."

"This is when music was music. What you know about this?" I asked, breaking into a hard-core Funky Chicken.

"Oh, gosh, Daddy! What are you doing?" She laughed.

"Can't hang?" I teased.

To my surprise, Alana began mocking my every move.

"Uh-oh. Is this a challenge?" I teased. "Check me out."

I did the Whop. The music changed. Keith Sweat's "I Want Her" came blasting through the speakers. Switched it up to the Cabbage Patch. Alana followed along. She smiled so hard, it looked like it hurt. We were cracking up, and we both worked up a sweat. The Roger Rabbit.

"Rhythm of the Night" by DeBarge led us into the Snake. I taught her the Kid 'n' Play to "She's Dope" by Bell Biv DeVoe.

"Daddy, I need some water," she said, begging for mercy. "I can't believe y'all danced like this in the eighties. It's more like a workout. I'm sweating."

I didn't care that I was sweating too. I enjoyed her being silly and acting a fool with me.

"I need some water too," I agreed as I led her off the empty dance floor.

The employees, Otis and a few patrons that had trickled in gave us a standing ovation.

Alana blushed as she graciously took the compliments.

"Two waters, please," I asked the bartender.

"These are on the house!" she said as she slapped the two bottles of Poland Spring on the bar.

"Hey, thanks," I panted, still winded from the dancing.

"I don't think I've ever had so much fun, Daddy!" Alana excitedly announced. She sprang into my arms and hugged me tightly.

We sat on the bar stools facing the floor. "The Place" had really come along. When Damon first brought me there, it was run-down and had wood paneling for walls and black leather sofas thrown around. Damon just liked the place because the drinks were cheap and Otis would guarantee a few laughs. It now had normal walls with high ceilings, painted beige, and the furniture was sleek mahogany wood, with plush brown cushions.

"So," Alana began, "what's up with you and Cassie?"

What *was* up with me and Cassie? I wondered. Whatever we had going on was all unspoken.

"Well, she's cool. We're kinda just getting to know each other, I guess. You know, taking it slow."

"You like her, don't you?" she asked, almost like it was a negative thing.

It didn't take much time for me to decide. "Yes, I do like her. I like her a lot. There's still so much I want to know about her, though."

"But why?" she whined. "Why?" she screamed, standing up in front of her stool.

She stared me down, really wanting an answer. Eyes looking wild and piercing through my face.

In an instant her mood had switched and our night was ruined.

"Alana, just calm down. I never said I was going to marry the woman, but I do like her."

"She's not all that, Dad! Why are you so easy? It's like every woman you meet has a chance with you. Don't you have any standards?" Her hands rested on her hips, like I owed her an explanation.

Fed up! I was fed up trying to wear kid gloves with her. Treating her like a six-year-old because of her depression. She kept crossing the line with me, and I was tired!

"Alana! I am the adult. You understand me? My love life is none of your damn business, and I'm tired of you always insulting the women I choose to have in my life. Did I insult that no-good Parker for standing you up? No, because I know that you care about him and that's all I need to know."

She stood there speechless. Eyes growing wider by the second. She wasn't used to me lashing out on her like this.

"You're almost an adult. Soon you're going to be moving away. I don't want to be alone, Alana. I want to get married. I want to have more kids. I want a life!" I screamed.

Otis came over and tapped me on the shoulder.

"Everything OK over here, 'Pretty Boy' Payton?"

"Everything's fine, Mr. Otis. It was nice to meet you again, but I'm leaving now," Alana faked in her most polite voice.

Her eyes were welled up with tears. Otis kissed her hand again and walked away.

"I hate you!" she screamed, and she turned to storm away.

I chased her out of the bar onto the street.

"Where are you going?" I yelled after her.

"None of your damn business!" she yelled back, breaking into a sprint down the street and cutting a corner. She was gone.

Chapter 32

Cassie

Mia was strapped up in her booster seat in the backseat of my car and we were singing Lloyd's "You" at the top of our lungs as we pulled out of our apartment complex to go to the pharmacy late that night. She knew every word and sang her little heart out too. I didn't find it strange when a car pulled out right behind us. Didn't find it strange when the car turned right when we turned right. I did, however, find it strange that at every stop the car behind me came to a sudden wheel-screeching stop. What the hell was this person doing? I stopped singing. Mia didn't miss a beat. She kept going, oblivious to the dumbass driver behind us.

Then the driver began feverishly flashing its lights at me, making it hard for me to see where I was going. Luckily, I hit the main street in no time. I turned left onto the Post Road and the person peeled off after me, cutting off the on-coming traffic and causing many horns to blow.

Now I was fully alarmed.

"Mia, do you have your seat belt on?" I asked frantically.

"Yes," she said before continuing her solo.

Adjusting my rearview mirror, I struggled to see who was following me so closely. It looked like a woman with a hood over her head wearing dark shades.

Fucking Summer . . .

Refusing to put my daughter in danger, I put on my hazard lights and slowly merged over to the right lane, while digging through my purse searching for my cell phone.

"Mommy, I thought we were going to get some cough medicine for me?" Mia asked, noticing our detour.

"We are, honey. Don't worry."

The car merged over to the right, along with us, putting on their hazards. My heart began to race. I was in the car with my six-year-old daughter and had no idea what this woman had up her sleeves. Couldn't find my damn phone! Knocked the entire purse over. Came to a complete stop. Turned on the lights and bent over to find my phone.

She began beeping her horn repeatedly. Her high beams were blinding me.

"Mommy, what's going on?" Mia asked, frightened, looking behind her toward the noise.

"Oh, nothing," I answered, trying to reassure her.

"I'm scared," she told me.

I ran out of excuses. I needed to find my damn phone.

She wanted me to get out of the car. Kept her high beams on. She wasn't such a monster, I thought as she kept beeping the horn. She knew Mia was in the car and wouldn't do anything too stupid, I hoped.

I knew I wouldn't have time to wait on the police, so I took matters into my own hands. She wanted me to get out of the car, so I got out of the car.

"I'll be right back," I told Mia. "I think the person behind me needs help."

I thrust the door open. I was tired of this desperate bitch messing with me, and she barked up the wrong tree, looking for trouble while I was with my daughter.

She saw me getting out and she got out too. She had on a baseball cap, hood over her head, and like I'd seen in the rearview mirror, she had on huge dark shades. She was petite.

"What the fuck do you want with me? My daughter's in the car, you psycho bitch!" I yelled.

She stood there, not backing down. Not speaking.

I screamed at her the entire time as I approached her. I got within arm's reach and she pulled my head down and kneed me in the face so quick and hard I barely knew what happened.

I lay on the side of the road, nosey motorists now slowing down to see what was going on. I was dizzy, my nose was bleeding. The bitch just stood over me, looking like the Grim Reaper. Then she hawked up a wad of phlegm and tried to spit at my face. My nose stung as I squirmed out of the way, right in time.

She tried to push me back down as I scrambled to my feet, but my adrenaline was in high gear. I grabbed her by the neck with one hand, drawing blood from the scratch marks that immediately appeared. I punched her in the face so hard that her glasses flew off her face and I knocked her ass backward to the ground. She got on all fours and frantically tried to find her sunglasses.

I kicked her in the back, causing her to fall back on the ground, face-first.

"Get up, bitch. Let me see your face! You want to fuck with me. Come on then!" I screamed. Every time she tried to get up, I kicked her back down. "Say something. Tell me to stay away from your man now! Well, he ain't your man anymore. He's mine." I kicked her again. She was crying. Pitiful.

"Fuck you!" she finally yelled back, refusing to turn around so I could see her face.

"No, fuck you. All this over a man? You're pitiful."

I looked over to my car. Saw Mia looking at me, crying hysterically. I snapped out of my rage. Realized the cops would be here any minute and there were hundreds of witnesses around. What the hell was I doing?

I ran back to my car, jumped in and peeled off.

Mia was hysterical. I didn't have any answers for her. I was hysterical. She had seen a side of me that she never should've seen. I raced home and ran upstairs with her in my arms. Locked the doors. Made sure the windows were locked.

"Mommy, what's wrong?" she asked, looking into my eyes for solace.

I didn't know what to tell her that would make sense. I told her, "Someone was trying to hurt us, so I had to protect us."

"Why would someone try to hurt us?"

I told her that some people were bad and needed to be put in jail. Nervously I paced around her room, trying to feed her lies that I knew she'd believe. She seemed satisfied after a while. She changed into her nightgown and I tucked her into bed.

"Thank you for protecting me tonight, Mommy," she said as I kissed her forehead.

I had never been involved in something so crazy before. Never had to fight over a man. No, I wasn't fighting over a man. I was fighting over my own security and protecting my daughter.

I sat on the edge of my bed, not able to relax. How could I sleep? Summer obviously knew where I lived because she followed me out of the parking lot. She could show up any minute.

God, I wanted to see her face. To be able to recognize her in the daylight. She had an advantage over me. She could roll up on me and I wouldn't even know it was her until she attacked me. I planted my face into my hands and began to cry. My world was sideways. I couldn't take it anymore.

I poured a glass of wine and sat on my couch in the dark. Sleep would not take me that night. *Poetic Justice* was on, so I watched that into the wee hours of the morning. Last time I checked the time, it was 4:00 A.M. Didn't hear anyone trying to break in. Heard no noise at all. But each time I heard a car whiz by outside, my eyes sprang open and my ears listened hard. Eventually sleep had its way with me and I drifted into an uncomfortable sleep.

When I woke up Saturday morning, the air stank. Mia slept late, and she never does. The apartment was quiet. I went straight to the bathroom, as I always do. The toilet water was running, like it always did. Washed my hands and the water wouldn't get warm. And there was no soap left. Something was off-kilter. Just wrong.

My vision was still blurry as I wobbled down the hall, back to my room. Flashbacks of the night before came in waves like a bad hangover. I was poking my head in to check on Mia when I heard a loud thud from the front of my apartment. Not a knock—a thud.

What the hell is that? I thought.

I could hear the pitter-patter of someone running down the hall.

Swinging the door open quickly, I was able to peer down the hall just in time to see the back of a black woman's head. She had a baseball cap on. There was a shoebox at my feet.

"Summer, I know it's you!" I screamed down the hall. "What do you want?" I yelped in frustration. I couldn't leave Mia alone in our apartment to go get in a scuffle with a psychopath yet again.

At my feet the box had an index card taped to the lid. In red paint it read: *You'll be next.* I lifted the shoebox. It was heavy. The bottom was soggy and left my hand wet.

I drew my hand back to see what the wetness was and realized my hand and the box were drenched in blood. The letters. They were written in blood, not paint. Bile rose from the back of my throat. The box dropped out of my hands. Hitting the floor, the top fell open and a sliced-up baby kitten fell out.

I ran back into my house, screaming. Woke Mia up.

"Mommy, what's wrong?" she yelled, running toward me.

"No, baby, just go back into your room. Mommy's OK," I yelled at her as I quickly turned back around to slam my front door shut and lock the door.

"Mommy, you're bleeding!" she screamed, now ferociously crying.

"No, baby, I was helping a hurt kitty. I'm OK. I just gotta call the doctor to have them come pick him up, OK? Just go in your room and close the door. I don't want you to see him, he's really hurt bad, OK?"

Her facial expression told me that she didn't buy my explanation, but she did as I said anyway.

Frantically I ran into my room and dialed 911.

"What's your emergency?"

"Someone was just at my door and they left a maimed cat in a shoebox. I'm alone with my daughter. Please send someone before they come back and hurt us."

She asked the appropriate questions and promised that someone was on the way.

This bitch is sick!

I called Payton. Ran to the bathroom to wash the blood off my hands. Couldn't keep still. Sitting on my bed, then walked to the front. Peeped out the window. Closed all the blinds. Double-checked that the door was locked.

"Payt, I think Summer was just here at my house. The police are on their way. Last night she followed me. We got in a fight. Now she left a dead fucking cat in a box with a note saying I was next! What the fuck?"

"She's not going to do anything dangerous. Damn it!" he yelled, frustrated. "Y'all had a fight?" he asked incredulously.

"She killed a baby cat, Payt! The bitch is insane! And she knows where I live, Payt! I have Mia to think about!"

"Look, Cassie, I'm so sorry you're caught in the middle of this. And I'm sorry for what she did. Any other time I would be over there in a flash, but I have to take Alana to her therapy session. Fuck!" he yelled clearly torn. "I promise

I'll be right over afterward, though. Is that OK with you?"

It pained me that he couldn't come be by my side during this craziness. After all, I was scared for my life because of his soured relationship! But then again, I reasoned, I wouldn't blow Mia's health off to be by his side either, so I let it go.

Called Tasha next.

"Good morning," she answered.

"Tash, get over here now! Don't get dressed. Don't brush your teeth. It's an emergency! Call me from your cell when you get in the car and I'll tell you what's going on, but get in the car now!"

Tasha wasted no time with good-byes. She just hung up and called me back less than three minutes later.

I sprinted to the bathroom to make sure the window was closed and locked.

"Girl, what the fuck is going on?" she screamed. "I'm in the car, burnin' rubber, girl!"

"I've been getting these threats. Payton has this crazy ex-girlfriend who's been fucking with me. The bitch was at my house this morning. She killed a cat and left it in a shoebox in front of my door, Tash!"

"I don't like the way!" she squealed.

"The cops are on the way, but I just need someone to be here with me. I'm buggin' out! OK, lemme go. Gotta go check on Mia. Hurry up!"

Mia was peacefully lying on her bed, watching cartoons. She gave me a weak smile. She was nervous but trying to be strong for me. She knew I'd come undone.

"Baby, the police are on the way to help the cat. Want a Pop-Tart or something? I want you to stay in your room the whole time, OK?"

"OK. No thank you. I'm not hungry yet, Mommy."

The police arrived first and Tasha was close behind. They collected the cat and the box in small plastic bags for evidence. I told them about the phone call and gave them the letter she'd left on my windshield.

Tasha escorted Freesia to Mia's room and told her to stay there.

The police's stay was brief. They gave me a few cards with numbers to call if she returned and asked me a million questions I couldn't answer. What does she look like? Height? What color was her baseball cap? Any team logo on the cap? Weight? Full name? After questioning, the police told me that, besides the box, nothing around the "area of discovery" had blood on it. They believed that perpetrator wore gloves.

"We'll contact you once we run the prints on the items you gave us, and you call us if you get any more information OK."

I thanked Sergeant Friedman and shook his hand. He and the other two officers left. The apartment was quiet again.

Tasha was making us some coffee in my kitchen. She'd already brought the girls bowls of cereal.

"Why didn't you tell me this woman was harassing you?" she asked, rightfully.

"Well, we haven't exactly been talking this week."

My nerves were starting to settle. I wrapped my slightly trembling hand around the warm mug and sipped the coffee slowly.

"I don't even want to talk about her anymore."

"Good," Tasha interjected. "'Cause I got an idea last night."

"What?" I wondered.

"We can write a tell-all book about Brice! He's trying to blow up using your song without your permission. What he did to me. All the times he cheated on you. You know people love those books telling celebrity business nowadays. I know it would blow up. We'd just have to wait until the perfect time to expose him. Right when he's at the top of the charts."

"That's a little evil, Tash. I don't know about that."

"And what he did to me wasn't evil? Think about it. You'll be able to get out of this apartment. Buy a nice house."

"I'm just going to sue him for what I am due, that's all."

"That too!"

I enjoyed the company Tasha was providing. I could always count on her to make me laugh. It was far better to be talking nonsense with her than to sit around, thinking about Summer invading my home while Mia and I slept at night.

We hung out all morning and ordered pizza and wings for lunch. We were waiting for the food to arrive when I got the call from Payton, and the day went back to hell. Something was wrong in his voice. Terribly, terribly wrong.

Chapter 33

Payton

When Alana ran off the night before, I hopped in the car and drove around for a while, looking for her. And, of course, I didn't find her. I figured she was running to Missy's, like she always did.

I regretted yelling at her the way I did, only because Parker had stood her up on the same night, so I added insult to injury. But she was getting on my damned nerves.

Got home at about midnight that night and called Missy to make sure Alana had arrived OK. Knew if I called Alana's cell, she wouldn't answer. But Missy swore on her mother that Alana was not there and she hadn't heard from her all night.

I called the police, but there was nothing they could do.

"She's seventeen years old. Probably just went to her boyfriend's house. Anyways, it hasn't been twenty-four hours yet. If you haven't heard from her by tomorrow night, give us a call back, Mr. Harris, and we can be of assistance."

I tried to care. I really did. Tried to care that she was missing. But I was exhausted. The police didn't care, and fuck it, I didn't care either. Her dramatic disappearing act would soon end and tomorrow she'd be "Suzy-fucking-Sunshine" again. I was getting off her sick roller coaster.

I needed to know what was going on in her head, so I went to her room. Rolled her mouse around and her computer came out of hibernation. But it was locked. Password protected. Went into her desk drawer. Paper. Pens. Couple papers scribbled on. Went to her dresser and opened the first drawer. It was her panty drawer. Closed it so fast I almost slammed my fingers up.

Her nightstand. I rifled through the top drawer where she kept her medicine and found nothing but the same half-empty bottle I'd checked days before. Closed that one and opened the bottom drawer. There was her birth control. Birth control? Why didn't I know she was on birth control already? Found a little jewelry box. Turned the box over, and I'll be damned if about twenty pills didn't fall out. *She hasn't been taking her medicine,* I realized. *She knows I am monitoring her and she's outsmarted me!* It certainly explained her recent insanity.

I stayed up late, but sleep took me at some point. I was awakened by Alana's footsteps creaking down the hall. It was 9:00 A.M. and she was just getting home.

She went straight to the bathroom and got in the shower. I still had my suit on. It was wrinkled and hanging loosely off my shoulders and waist. I didn't have enough energy to shower. Alana's therapy session was at 10:00 A.M.; I would go just as I was. I was in the half bath downstairs when I felt my phone vibrating on my hip.

It was Cassie. Summer had killed a fucking cat and threatened to kill her. I was numb to that bullshit at the moment. Not that I didn't care, just had to get Alana to therapy and address the fact that she hadn't been taking her medicine. I would go straight to Cassie's house to take care of her after Alana's therapy session, though.

"Good morning, Daddy. Sorry about last night. You ready to go? Why are you still in the same clothes from last night? Gross," she cheerily stated.

I couldn't. Wouldn't reprimand her for last night. *She's ill*, I reminded myself. And she hadn't been taking her medication.

I noticed a small gash on her hand as she reached for the light switch to the kitchen.

"What happened to your hand?" I asked, alarmed.

She drew it back quickly.

"Uh, this? This . . . I . . . uh . . . I cut my hand last night. I went to . . . Parker's house . . . last night . . . We argued," she stammered.

"Did he put his hands on you?" I screamed.

"No, Daddy. Look, it's OK. Let's just get outta here. Aren't you going to change?"

"No, I'm fine. Did he put his hands on you?" I asked again.

"No!" she screamed. "I got mad at *him*. I tried to hit *him*. He was defending himself when he pushed me down. I went to confront him about standing me up, and when I got there, he was with another chick!" she cried, breaking into tears. "Let's go!" she yelled, eager to get to therapy.

I wanted to sit in on the session this time around. Had to get to the bottom of her not taking her medication and what happened between her and Parker.

"Yeah, let's go!" I agreed.

The sunlight hit me as we sauntered out of the house and I realized how raggedy I looked. Alana took off toward the car, holding a package in her hand and wearing all black.

"Can you stop by the mailbox at the corner so I can mail this?" she asked, holding the padded envelope out.

I nodded my head. "What's that?"

"My financial-aid package," she dryly replied.

We headed to the corner. She got out slowly and dropped the package off and got back in.

The world was moving quickly around us. Our world inside the car was in slow motion. Alana plugged her ears with her iPod. My mind was racing. I tried to focus on my daughter. Her illness. But my mind wandered over to Cassie's house, where I envisioned her pulling her hair out about Summer's antics. Then

Summer sitting in her apartment, laughing, feeling good about the drama she'd stirred up. Then it flip-flopped back to Alana and Parker and what the hell happened last night.

Beep! My tires came to a screeching halt. I'd almost hit the car in front of me when it stopped at the red light.

My heart skipped a beat. Alana didn't flinch.

We pulled up to the doctor's office and Alana skipped ahead of me, like she always did, and escaped behind closed doors with Dr. Weinstein.

Molly was taken aback by my appearance.

"Tough week, Mr. Harris?" she asked.

"Truer words have never been spoken." I sighed, walking past her desk into Dr. Weinstein's office.

The graying doctor greeted me with a nod of the head.

"I want to sit in today," I announced.

"Daddy, no!" Alana pleaded.

"You don't have a choice. I'm sitting in on the session today. I want to know why you haven't been taking your medicine!" I yelled.

Alana sprang up from her chair, her eyes widened like saucers.

"Daddy!" she yelled, almost like a question.

"Yes, I looked through your drawers, and your jewelry box was filled with pills that you should've been taking every day."

"I can't believe you went through my stuff!" she screamed, immediately turning red. Her hands were shaking. She stood there, embarrassed, like she was suddenly naked in front of a room full of people.

Instantly I felt guilty for upsetting her so much. And it was then that I noticed the scratch marks on her neck too.

"What happened to your—" I started.

"Mr. Harris, I think—" Dr. Weinstein said, trying to interrupt, but I talked right over her.

"Sugar, look, I was just concerned. You've been acting so weird lately. I wanted to know what was up, that's all. You know you can't just stop taking your pills like that."

"Those pills make me feel like a different person! I have no personality. No sense of humor. I feel like my soul is standing outside of me looking at the real me and wondering who the hell I am! I'm not crazy and I don't need no fucking pills to help me be normal! I'm your daughter and you should know that."

The wound on her hand began to bleed on the carpet. She grasped it sharply and let out an agonizing scream.

"You OK?" I rushed toward her, but she drew back.

"Don't touch me!" Alana demanded. "Please just let me have ten minutes alone with Dr. Weinstein. Please?" she begged, now bawling.

"Sounds like a fair compromise to me, Mr. Harris," Dr. Weinstein agreed, raising her eyebrow at me in silent reprimand.

I looked Alana in her desperate eyes and walked away, closing the door behind me.

Molly brought her curvy hips from around the desk and sat next to me on the suede love seat. My head was cradled in my hands as I stared down at my tapping foot.

"Wanna talk about it?" she asked, placing her hand on my knee. I was so shaken up by everything else going on, it took me a while to realize that in all the time I'd known her, she'd never gotten personal with me.

My expression told her that I was confused. Taken aback.

She blushed. Looked away. Covered her mouth with her hand and giggled.

"Not really," I admitted. My burden was too heavy to lay before this woman I barely knew. "I mean, I would, but—but it's just too much."

"Maybe we could talk one day over dinner?" she suggested.

It didn't take long to digest what she was doing this time; she was flirting with me. My body wasn't capable of knowing how to react to it either. My body decided it wanted to laugh.

Her body decided the same.

"Yeah, maybe that would be nice," I said.

"I actually just broke up with my boyfriend a couple days ago, so my mind's a little messed up now too. He's taking the breakup pretty hard. Making it a bigger deal than it needs to be."

"I can relate to that one, more than you know. That's kind of the reason I'm a mess today," I told her.

If I had to choose one defining moment in my

life—just one moment—this was it. Not sharing a common bond with Molly, but the moment right after.

"Mr. Harris!" the shrill voice yelled repeatedly.

Molly and I both sprang from our seats and busted through the door to Dr. Weinstein's office.

In that moment my life was defined.

Dr. Weinstein's legs were on her chair, pulled into her chest. She was shaking. A child afraid of a beating.

"Dr. Weinstein!" Molly yelled as she ran over to embrace her.

"Where's Alana?" I screamed, frozen.

Molly's eyes were wide, mouth open.

"Where's my daughter?" I screamed.

Dr. Weinstein pointed to the window.

The window was open.

Running the small distance to the window drained me of all energy. The sight drained me of all desire to live.

Alana was sprawled on the pavement below. Her legs awkwardly bent in different directions. A pool of blood encircled her head.

Dr. Weinstein explained, "She just . . . she just jumped."

Chapter 34

Cassie

The news of Alana's suicide shook me. I cried instantly. The pain in Payton's voice slapped me in the face. And it stung. Stung like nothing had ever stung before. Then for a fleeting moment I selfishly thought of the possibility of losing Mia.

"Cassie, she's not here anymore. My Sugar's gone," he'd said.

Before I could ask, he whispered, "Committed suicide."

"Do you want me to come over?" I asked. Tasha and Free were spending the night at my house, so I was prepared to run out to be with him. Console him.

"I . . . I need . . . I just want to be alone tonight," he told me.

I didn't hear from him the rest of the night. Tried calling to check on him but got no answer. I'd grown to care about Payton and prayed that he wouldn't harm himself that night.

When he called me at six on Sunday morning, I was overwhelmingly happy to hear from him, despite the time. I sat straight up in my bed and clutched the phone tight to my ear. He frowned through his words.

"Can you come over now?" he asked. "I'm not going to make it much longer like this."

"Sure—"

"The walls are closing in on me. Haven't eaten. The thought of eating makes me want to vomit. Haven't slept since Friday night. My eyes have sand in them. But when I close my eyes, all I can see is her. On the ground. Facedown. Was her life that bad, Cassie? I failed her!" he screamed.

"Payt, I'm on my way. Just hang in there until I get there."

Hopping around on one leg to put on my jeans, I nudged Tasha to let her know I was leaving. She hummed an OK through her slumber.

Payton's house was in shambles. I knocked, but he didn't answer. The door was unlocked, so I let myself in. He'd ripped off the curtains, leaving two windows bare. The rays of sun were shining brightly on the debris splattered about the floor. I stepped through the rubble. Passing over old pictures, candles, clothes, figurines and paintings. The walls were naked. He'd smashed everything. A gaping hole was toward the bottom of the wall that separated the living room from the kitchen. He must've kicked through it.

"Payt?" I yelled softly, toward the stairs.

"I'm up here," I heard faintly.

I weaved my way through the mess he'd made

in his rage until I reached the bottom of the stairwell. I paused for a moment to admire the picture of Alana that lay there. She must've been six or seven. Her two bottom teeth missing. Smiling so wide. A loosely wound ponytail lay tilted to the side of her head and held together with a bright green bow. Her shirt was pink and white polka dots. Pink-white-and-bright-green hair bows adorned her hair, which was tousled and dry; not a drop of grease to help the cause. A daughter prepared for picture day by her single father.

My weak legs made it to the top of the stairwell quickly.

"On the left," I heard him direct me.

Payton was sitting on the edge of his bed. He didn't look at me as I entered the room. I stepped softly toward him. The scene sent an overwhelming amount of sadness into my heart. The room was dark. Heavy curtains pulled tightly closed, shunning the sunlight. He was wearing a wrinkled tan suit and unbuttoned baby blue shirt. Hadn't slept or changed his clothes in days.

I kneeled before him, in between his legs. He wouldn't open his eyes. I touched his eyelids softly. Rubbed my hand over his head.

There was nothing I could say. I couldn't understand his pain. So I kept quiet. Planted my head on his chest and wrapped my arms around his neck. His clothes smelled stale. Not rank, just stale with the hint of dried sweat. But I held on to him despite that. It didn't bother me.

It was quiet, still, eerie. He hadn't moved. Looked up and his eyes were still closed. Didn't want to open them and face his new world. A world in which he was no longer a father. A proud father.

My knees were starting to burn from kneeling so long. I don't know where the words came from, as I wasn't a religious person, per se. Hadn't been to church since Johnny was a boy, but the first word I said after being there for about half an hour was "'God.'"

"God, there are many mysteries in life we don't understand. The death of a child being one of the most puzzling. Save Payton from blaming himself and others. Help him loosen the bonds of anger, bitterness and hurt. Heal his wounds, Lord. Help us to see that although Alana is no longer with us physically, she is close to us still. And will always be. Amen."

"Amen," Payton said in agreement. "Thank you," he said, forcing a weak smile. His eyes finally opened and looked into mine. Tears defiantly streamed down his face.

I wiped them away but told him through tears of my own, "Let it out. It's OK to feel what you're feeling."

I got off my knees and stood before him. He grabbed my waist and pulled me into him. Burying his head into my stomach, he cried. Hard. He held me too tightly; it hurt. But I didn't dare budge.

He finally released my hips and burrowed his head into his hands.

"I'll be downstairs," I whispered.

He nodded and fell backward on his bed, leaving his feet firmly planted on the ground before him.

Downstairs I hung his pictures back on the wall, threw the destroyed items in the trash and put all the scattered pictures in a stack on his coffee table. Opened up the windows. Windexed. Dusted. Swept. Took the garbage out. Vacuumed. It was about an hour later and Payton was still upstairs.

Called Tash to check on the girls, but they were still asleep.

"Make sure you keep the doors and windows locked, Tash. Just in case that crazy bitch decides to come back," I told her.

"No doubt. How's Payton?"

I told her how he wasn't talking and had trashed his own house.

"Can you blame him?" she sympathized.

"Not at all," I replied. "So I'm going to just chill for a few more hours, but I should definitely be home around noon, OK?"

"That's cool. I might take the girls to the movies or something. They ain't gonna drive me crazy up in your tiny-ass apartment," she joked. "So don't worry about rushing home. Payton needs you."

I ended up staying for three more hours. First I went back upstairs to check on Payton; he was asleep. I wanted to be there to say good-bye when he woke up. Looked briefly down the hall toward Alana's room and got immediate shivers.

I had only met her once, just when she came to Tasha's to babysit the girls while Tasha and I went to Vanilla Sky. She was nice enough in the five minutes we'd spent together. Pretty too. I remembered her amber eyes were stunning. She had long, light brown hair with golden streaks. Not bleached, but kissed by the sun in all the right places—golden. Remembering her strong cheekbones and sharp, petite nose, she had similar features to that of her father. But the eyes and hair, that was from her mother, for sure. She was polite. In our brief introduction she had told me that she was attending NYU in the fall, but she didn't know what her daddy was going to do without her.

She'd said jokingly, "He thinks he wants his space. Wants me outta here. As soon as I'm gone, he'll want me home like every weekend. He's not fooling me."

We laughed. I smiled thinking back on the one conversation we'd shared in her short time here. She seemed so happy, I thought.

Although I'd never been to Payton's house before, I didn't feel like an outsider. I turned the radio on.

"That was 'Shy Girl' by newcomer Brice Morgan . . ." I heard.

I clicked the off button so damn fast, I almost pushed the radio off the shelf.

Decided to nestle on the couch and watch TV, instead. But soon sleep crept up on me and had its way with me.

I was awakened by Payton standing over me, calling my name.

"Hey, you," I groggily replied, wiping my eyes.

Although he'd gotten a little sleep, his eyes were still glazed with red. Bags under his eyes told me that his sleep wasn't sound. It was a violent rest, polluted with gory visions and morbid acts.

"Thank you. You didn't have to do all this," he stated, referring to his clean house.

"No, it's OK. The least I could do. Wanna eat something?" I asked, starting to feel hunger in my own stomach.

"I guess I should," he said with a shrug. "Probably isn't much in there to cook, though."

"Oh, please. I don't cook anyway. Well, I can. Just don't like to. I can order like a pro, though," I said, trying to get a laugh out of him.

He smiled politely and told me where I could find a bunch of menus in his kitchen.

"Probably should take a shower, huh?" he said, looking down at his run-down suit.

"OK, so by the time you finish, the food should be here."

I ordered the herb chicken, lasagna and a house salad from Pellicci's for us to share.

Just like I thought, Payton emerged downstairs as I was paying the deliveryman. He looked handsome in his basketball shirt and wife-beater, despite the turmoil going on inside him.

I spread the food out on his dining-room table and we sat across from each other. He wouldn't look at me. Poked around in his food. Took a bite here and there.

"Wanna talk about it?" I asked, halfway through my meal.

"Not really, Cassie. I'm still trying to put it all together. Not yet."

Chapter 35

Payton

Cassie left that afternoon and I didn't feel any better. While I appreciated her thoughtfulness, there was nothing that could lift my spirits. Not a damn thing. There are things that you think could never happen to you. And there are things that are just never supposed to happen. Children are not supposed to die before their parents. They're just not!

The rest of my afternoon was spent sitting in my bedroom, lights off, door closed. Sleep did not come, even though I was exhausted. I stared at the ceiling. And stared some more.

Thought back to her childhood when she was always happy. Dr. Weinstein didn't recognize any symptoms of her bipolar disorder until shortly after she turned fourteen. Back then it was more widely known as manic depression. Before then, though, she'd been so happy all the time. Her biggest letdowns were not being able to wear a skirt every day of the week, and not being able to eat sweets when she wanted. Her grades were good. Her life was good, even though her mother was gone.

When she was little, we'd have an ongoing rivalry. Some nights before bed, she'd say, "Daddy, I love you this much," then stretch her arms open as far as she could.

I'd say "And I love you this much!" stretching my longer arms from side to side, showing more love.

"Not fair," she'd pout. "One day my arms are going to be longer than yours and then we'll see who loves who more," she'd boast.

Happy.

Fourteen came and happiness dissipated. We still had our good times too, though, but overall that's when her attitude kicked in and the mood swings started.

My mind froze on the earlier half of her life. So many things we'd conquered together: chicken pox, strep throat, poison ivy, ice-skating, the tooth fairy, learning to swim.

I knew I had to tell Keisha that she had one less child now, but it would be hard. Not that it would affect her all that much, but I guess she deserved to know. I wouldn't do it over the phone—had to be a face-to-face conversation.

I dragged myself over to the phone and dialed her number from the letter I'd kept.

"Hello," she happily answered. Again her cheery disposition angered me.

"Keisha, can you meet me back at Dunkin'

Donuts tomorrow? I'm going to sign those papers."

"Oh, so what changed your mind, huh?" she asked cockily. I could picture her snapping her neck and placing her hand on her hip, expectantly.

"Look, Keisha. Are you going to be there or not? I don't have time for your bullshit right now. For real," I fired, knocking the cheeriness right out of her.

"I'll be there," she agreed.

I hung up in her face, not giving her the decency of a salutation.

Her ugly attitude gave me a needed distraction from my plaguing thoughts of Alana. Propelled me to my feet. I burned tracks in the carpet from pacing back and forth. Didn't think to turn on the air conditioner. Instead, I roasted—letting the sweat penetrate my clothes.

Keisha's shit didn't distract me for long. Soon my daughter's face was all I saw. Her voice all I heard.

Dr. Weinstein had given me her home number. Told me to call her when I was up to it. I wanted to know what happened in that room. Wanted to know her final words. Needed to know why.

I dialed her number and held my breath until she answered.

"Dr. Weinstein, it's Payton Harris. You . . . you said I could call if . . . if I wanted to talk?"

"Of course, Mr. Harris. I just want to express

how sorry I am that this happened. I haven't personally experienced a death of a child, but I can only imagine what you must be going through."

"Yeah, I'm not doing too well," I agreed. "So what happened in there? Why'd she jump?"

"I'm still trying to wrap my mind around that same question. Why'd she jump? She walked in the office, smiling. Said, 'Good Morning, Dr. Weinstein' and had a seat on the chair. I asked her how her week was. 'Been better,' she said with a shrug."

Dr. Weinstein paused. Took a deep breath. It was hard for her to rehash this story.

"Sorry," she offered. "Never seen someone take her own life in front of me before. But, OK, um, so she wanted to talk about you. Said you and she had two big fights this week. I was asking her what caused the blowouts. But she ignored that question. 'Parker was supposed to meet Payton last night,' she said. 'Ain't that some funny shit? Parker, meet Payton.' She laughed. She wouldn't stop laughing.

"That's when things just got strange. In an instant her laughter turned into crying. Her body started shaking. First her hands, then soon everything was jerking uncontrollably. I—I should've called you in then!" Dr. Weinstein yelled. She was now crying.

"But—but I thought I had it under control. If I had just called you in the office right then, maybe your daughter would still be here!"

On the other line I didn't breathe. Didn't move. Somehow my brain instructed my mouth and tongue to say, "Don't blame yourself."

"I got up and put my arms around her. Told her to relax a little bit, so we could talk. And she did! Calmed right down, but her eyes were stuck wide open. She stared at the window. Didn't blink once. 'Payton wants to meet Parker,' she repeated in a low, husky voice. Didn't take her eyes off the window. I thought she was just avoiding eye contact with me. Didn't think she was thinking about jumping.

"'I need some fresh air. Can I open your window?' she asked. I told her, sure, go ahead. Wanted her to be as comfortable as possible, since she was so upset. 'Payton wants to meet Parker,' she continued repeating. I asked, 'What does that mean?' She ignored me. Laughed it off. 'Payton wants to meet Parker,' she repeated as she walked over and opened the window. She stuck her head out and took a deep breath. Laughed again. Then she quickly stuck one leg out of the window.

"I stood up and went for my phone to call Molly, But she whispered hard, 'If you call Molly, I will jump. If you scream for my dad, I will jump.' I tried calling her bluff. Told her, 'Well, aren't you just going to jump anyway? So why does it matter if I call them or not?' I moved closer to her and she quickly pulled her other leg over, sitting on the edge of the windowsill. 'I know whether I'm going to jump or not, but you don't. And if I jump because you did something that I asked you not to, then that'll be on your conscience forever, now wouldn't it? Now don't come any closer to me!" she directed.

"She'd trapped me in a proverbial corner. If I called you, she would've jumped right away. If I didn't, I had the chance to coax her off the ledge.

"'Why do you keep repeating that, Alana? You don't want Parker to meet your dad?' I asked. 'You don't get it, do you? No one gets it!' she yelled, but careful not to yell too loudly. 'What? What am I not getting, Alana? Come on down from there and tell me. Please?' I begged.

"'Don't worry. In a few days everyone will get it. Everyone will understand why I had to do this.'"

"That was it, Mr. Harris. She closed her eyes and titled forward. She went down quietly, no screaming."

I thought I was going to get answers, but now I was more confused than before I called Dr. Weinstein.

Ain't that some funny shit? "Payton wants to meet Parker."

Chapter 36

Cassie

My mind was cloudy at work the next morning. Nothing at work made sense. Much like everything outside of work. There was something about the death of a child, even if not your own, that just shook up the universe and made everything unaligned.

At home our morning went off without a hitch. No murdered cats, no threatening notes, no prank phone calls. Got Mia off to camp on time, but walked into work fifteen minutes late. The norm.

But unlike the many times when I was able to slip through the door and take the phone off overnight mode, the office manager was standing behind my desk with her chubby arms folded across her man-chest.

"Were you going to call and let someone know you'd be late?" she remarked with a smirk.

"I'm late? Didn't know. Sorry," I replied in my nastiest tone possible. I walked around her and placed my purse on my desk. "Excuse me," I said, letting her know that she was in my way.

She walked off in a huff. *Whatever,* I thought.

I shook my mouse around and woke my computer out of sleep mode. But the screen was not the usual log-in screen. I always locked my computer and password protected. *Someone's been on my shit,* I thought.

The switchboard began lighting up. Couldn't find my earpiece to answer it. Too late, the call went into voice mail. *Where's my earpiece?*

I opened up my e-mail and it was filled with a week's worth of mess that I'd have to catch up on in a day. Taking time off from work was never worth it.

I fished around in and on my desk for my earpiece and couldn't find it anywhere. Frustrated, I left my desk and went to the dingy break room to get a cup of coffee. I had no friends at work. Was never invited to happy hour. I just worked there and picked up my pay stubs every first and fifteenth.

So when I entered the break room, I wasn't surprised when all I got from the five people standing around was a "good morning." No one asked if I was feeling OK, even though I'd just taken the previous week off for what they thought were health reasons.

"Good morning," I returned.

I missed about four more calls that morning and realized there were several time-sensitive e-mails that went unanswered last week. "Oh, well" was my attitude. It was strange to me that when I was actually in the office, no one ever asked anything of me.

I couldn't give much thought to the stupid crap I'd come back to at work—too much personal stuff going on. I was pondering getting a security system installed in my apartment. Maybe at least getting some of those window alarms they have at Home Depot. Summer didn't seem like she was going to give up harassing me anytime soon. And I didn't plan on ending whatever it was that me and Payton had going on anytime soon either. So she and I had a problem.

Sipping on my coffee, I logged on to homedepot.com to look around for some window alarms. For the time being that would have to do, because I didn't have any money for a security system.

I really hadn't had time to seriously think about Tasha and Brice, with all the other craziness going on. But being back at my boring job made me start thinking about things. I couldn't shake the fact that I didn't quite believe Tasha's story. I couldn't put my finger on it, but something just wasn't right. I replayed the whole scene from Brice's foyer in my mind, over and over again. Analyzed everything that was said and the body language. Although they were both guilty, Tasha was fidgety and seemed more angry. Brice just seemed confident and ready to confront the issue. No matter how many indiscretions Brice has had on me over the years, I knew he really loved me to the best of his ability.

Then I dissected the story Tasha had fed me about him taking her home that night she was intoxicated and raping her. Brice is the biggest ladies' man out there and it really struck me strange that he had to take advantage of Tasha to have sex with her. Then I tried remembering that weekend that I went to visit my grandfather in Boston. When I returned, was there anything strange about their interactions? It was so long ago that I couldn't remember anything. Damn it!

"Having fun?" the bitch Amanda said, noticing I was surfing around on homedepot.com. "Do you even hear the phone ringing?"

Damn, I hadn't heard it, because my mind was consumed with Brice and Tasha.

"Look," I began humbly, "I have a lot of personal issues right now. And a good friend of mine's daughter just—"

"Cry me a river," she interrupted.

My head snapped back and the little black girl from Custer Street appeared. She would come out from time to time when the opportunity presented itself. I could not be held responsible for her actions either.

"Who the fuck do you think you're talking to like that? I am not your child. I'm a grown-ass woman with a child of my own." I jumped up from my chair and put my hands on my hips. "You have no idea the shit I'm dealing with right now!"

"Nor do I care," she said, not cowering away

from the confrontation. "You are paid to do a job here. When you actually grace us with your presence, your work is half-assed and you're on the phone or surfing the Internet. Then you're constantly taking days off and leaving early. Coming in late. You act like we owe you something. All we owe you is two paychecks a month."

"I work my ass off for this place!" I defended myself.

"No, you don't. You do the bare minimum, as to not get fired. While you were gone, I had IT log me into your computer. Looks like all you do is send personal e-mails all day."

I could see where this was heading. She wanted me to lose my temper and go storming out. I knew better, I had a mouth to feed. She would have to fire me so that I could collect unemployment. So I stood there quietly. Sent the little girl from Custer Street back home.

"So what are you saying?" I asked. The pit of my stomach felt like I'd swallowed a bowling ball. I had no savings. We were living paycheck to sorry-ass paycheck.

"Do you want to be here?" she asked. She was trying to get me to quit.

"What are you saying, Amanda?"

"What do you want to do?"

I wasn't giving in. Our standoff had created a lot of attention in the office. I could feel the people passing by and staring.

"Amanda, I'm not playing this game with you.

If you're done talking, then I'm going to get back to work."

I turned around nonchalantly and sat back at my desk. Amanda didn't budge; she was still standing over me.

"Don't you turn your back to me!" Amanda yelled in frustration.

The girl inside me from Custer Street threatened to come back out and punch this chick in her face. Talking like she's royalty or something. But I told her to fall back.

I wanted to stand up to Amanda and defend myself, but she was right. I did do a half-assed job. I just didn't think anyone noticed or cared. I did a half-assed job, because all I ever wanted to do was sing, not sit up in somebody's office answering phones.

Finally she surrendered the words she couldn't wait to utter, "You're fired. Please leave, now!"

"Gladly," I replied, snatching Mia's picture and stuffing it into my purse as I walked out with my head up.

But as soon as I hit the elevator, I cried like a baby. What the hell was I going to do for work?

Work. Exactly! Tasha's story was completely made-up I realized on the elevator ride down. They'd slept together, all right—they both agreed on that, but Brice did not rape Tasha. I remember now that Tasha and I were both working the night shift at CVS around then, and the only way I was able to get the night off to see my grandfather was because Tasha covered my shift. The shift was from 8:00 P.M. to 1:00 A.M. and she would've had to go straight from rehearsal, so there was no way in hell she went out with Brice after rehearsal and got drunk and had to be taken home.

I stepped off the elevator, feeling deflated, but at the same time realizing the betrayal was deeper than Brice. Tasha had lied to me about how they slept together. Why would she lie? I called her right away as I walked through the parking lot to my car.

"Hey, girl!" she answered.

"Tash, I was just thinking about what you told me about you and Brice the other day."

There was quiet on the other end of the phone. So I continued.

"It took me a minute to realize it, but that time I went to Boston, you covered my shift at CVS, remember?"

"Yeah—yeah, I did cover your shift, but it happened after I left."

She didn't even sound convincing. It was pitiful.

"Tasha, you're lying! You told me y'all went out right after rehearsal and he spent the night, and the next morning you woke up and kicked his ass for what he did to you."

I'd made it to my car but couldn't get in. I threw my purse on the trunk and stood there, boldly yelling into my cell phone. "Tasha! Do you have anything to say for yourself?"

"Cassie, I'm sorry. You're right. I—I just didn't want to lose you a friend. I thought if I told you it happened without my permission, then we'd still have a chance to be friends. Cassie, the last thing I want to do is lose you. You're my sister."

"No, you're not my sister. My sister would not have me believe that the man that I loved—off and on for a decade—the man I had a child with, was some sort of monster that would rape my best friend!"

"OK, OK, Cassie, lemme tell you what really happened t-then," she stammered.

"No, it's OK. We're through. I don't need this right now. And you're a lying bitch. Why would I believe you at this point?"

"What about the girls?" she asked, referring to Mia and Freesia.

The question was like a stab in the heart, because they were inseparable. The girls loved each other, like Tasha and I loved each other.

"I'm sorry, but they're still young. They'll meet new friends and forget about each other soon enough."

With that said, I pressed the end button and got into my car and cried for at least an hour.

Chapter 37

Payton

"Look, man, here's the deal," Damon said. "Just give me the power of attorney over the arrangements and I'll take care of everything. You can't just refuse to deal with it. It has to be done. Alana deserves the best, man. She was my daughter too."

Damon had given me a full day to get my mind right before coming to visit. He was on duty when 911 was called for Alana and responded to the scene. The death had hit him almost as hard as it did me. He had to be dragged away from the scene in the same manner that I was—kicking and screaming, throwing punches at the air.

He had come over to the house to try to force me to start preparing for Alana's funeral. Honestly, I fully trusted him to handle everything, and he was right—I just couldn't do it.

"A'ight, man. You sure, though?"

"Man, c'mon, don't insult me. It'll be my

pleasure. Did you take a shower today? You look like shit," he remarked.

"Na, but I will. Gotta go meet up with Keisha later and deliver the news. And sign those divorce papers and all that."

"Aw, man. That's going to be rough. Keep your head up, my dude."

"Yeah, I'ma try. I'm thinking about moving outta here too. This place is just too big for me, and too many memories are here, na'mean? It's too fucking quiet around here, man. This shit is haunting me!"

He was silent, but he nodded his head in agreement.

"A'ight, well, let me get outta here. See if I can pull some strings and get this power of attorney paperwork drawn up real quick."

"Thanks, brah," I said, giving him a pound.

I dressed quickly, not caring what I threw on, and hurried out the door. It was almost time to meet up with Keisha.

I wasn't nervous, just anxious. Wanted to get it over with.

Grabbing my keys off the coffee table, I ran sloppily through the foyer and out the door. Once I reached my front lawn, I saw Summer standing by my car.

Shit!

"Summer, not now!" I yelled.

"No, Payton, listen to me," she begged, side-stepping me, blocking me from entering my car.

"I—I heard about Alana. I just want to say I'm sorry. See if there's anything you need?"

Her eyes glowed with sincerity.

"Thanks, now if you'll excuse me," I said, gesturing for her to move aside.

"How are you handling everything?" she asked.

I flew off the handle. She'd had it coming for a while. And after what she did to Cassie on Saturday, her evil ass was sitting up in my face, talking to me about my daughter.

"None of your goddamn business, Summer. Leave me alone, you crazy-ass bitch! Leave me alone and leave my girl alone too."

My girl?

"What the hell did I do to deserve this?" She immediately started with her tears.

"Good riddance, Summer. Get the fuck away from my property!"

She still hadn't budged from in front of my car door. I picked her up under her arms and moved her to the side. She started kicking and punching me, but I couldn't feel anything. Someone could've shot me in the balls right then and I wouldn't have flinched.

I jumped in the car and headed to Dunkin' Donuts.

Keisha was already there when I arrived, sipping her coffee and eating a donut.

"Hey," she said as I took the seat across from her. "You gonna get a coffee or something?"

"Na," I told her. "You got those papers?"

"Of course." She smiled as she handed them to me from her oversized bag.

I angrily scribbled my name on the line provided. The moment was here. I had to say it. Had to say it out loud.

"Alana's dead, Keisha."

She smiled. Took a sip of her coffee. "What are you talking about, Payton?"

"I'm talking about our daughter's dead, Keisha. I'm not bullshitting!"

Immediately her nose flared.

"What do you mean? How? When?"

I wasn't ready for this. Wasn't ready for this to be real.

I shared the circumstances of Alana's death. She stared into her coffee. A couple weak tears escaped her eyes.

"I'm sorry," she finally said, biting her bottom lip.

"Yeah, me too. So we're done here, right?" I asked, more than ready to leave.

"Wait, when are the services for her?"

"Her godfather will give you a call when the plans are made."

I got up to leave.

"Wait!" she begged. "Don't you want to know what happened to me that night? Why I couldn't return home? I've felt so guilty about this for years and now she's . . . she's gone."

I sat back down.

As much as I didn't want to be in her presence, that question had plagued me for seventeen years. I wanted to know what happened that a mother could abandon her family. Keisha had obviously shed all the tears she was going to shed over the baby she abandoned at six months old.

"So in my letter I told you how I'd developed the addiction to crystal meth and was in a relationship with a guy named Larry."

She waited for a response. I gave her a blank stare back.

"So that night I met up with Larry, like I always did. But that night there was two other men in the car with him. Larry told me that he was in trouble. Said that I'd smoked up too much of his shit and he had people to pay, and no way to pay them. They had run out of ideas for a low-key way to get the money they needed and it was on me to come up with an idea. But they didn't let me come up with an idea—they already knew what the plan was. I was just a pawn in their plan.

"We pulled up to my mother's house after midnight. Larry reminded me that I told him about all the jewelry my mother had inherited from her mother a few months earlier. They were making me rob my mother. I begged him to leave her alone. Begged them to drive off. Screamed for them to pull off. Threatened to tell the cops. 'Bitch, I'll kill you. Now get your ass out the car and open the door,' he yelled.

"I got out of the car and led them into my

mother's house. Larry handed me a couple rocks of ice and told me to have a little fun while I waited."

Now she cried uncontrollably. The conversation we were having was way too deep for an afternoon at Dunkin' Donuts. Cried rivers about her own demons, but only shed courtesy tears for her daughter's death.

"So you let them rob your mother? That was pretty low."

"That's all they were supposed to do. That's all they said they were going to do, Payton. But . . . but they brutally raped her. And I heard it. Knew what was going on to my own damn mother and I ignored it. I smoked my ice and tuned out her screaming. Tuned out the sound of their fists breaking her bones. Tuned out everything. The louder, more rowdy, they became, the harder I hit the ice.

"I sat back and did drugs while three men raped my mother in the next room, Payton!"

Didn't know what to say. I was shocked and disgusted. But I had no sympathy for her. Since I was in a nasty-ass mood anyway, I didn't hold my tongue.

"I wondered all these years what type of person would desert their husband and little baby girl. I'm glad I stayed around to hear that story. Now I have my answer. All it takes is someone like you. A disgusting, selfish bitch that would let men gangbang her mother for her own satisfaction. It all makes sense now.

"I just told you that your firstborn child committed suicide. She was suffering from an illness that had no cure. I don't give a fuck about what you did to your mother. All I care about is what you did to our daughter. Her blood will be on your hands forever. Live with that!"

I left her there, wallowing in her self-pity. I had my own pity party to throw.

Chapter 38

Cassie

The next morning I dropped Mia off at camp and then went to Costco to stock up on some essentials. I knew the next few months would be tough for Mia and me. Spent almost two hundred dollars in there, which was a lot for our newly downsized budget.

As I struggled up the stairs, I noticed a bouquet of flowers at my doorstep. After dropping a few boxes in the house, I went to see who they were from. The roses were from Brice. It didn't surprise me at all.

Unpacked the rest of the car before reading the card from the flowers. *He must know that I'm hearing him singing my song all over the radio,* I thought.

The phone rang. It was him.

"Did you get my flowers?" he asked.

"I did. And I thought you should know that when I first spoke to Tasha about what happened between you two, she fed me this story about you taking advantage of her one night when she was drunk, and I believed her. That's why I haven't had much to say to you lately. But I realized after I had time to really think about it, it was all a lie."

"That was stupid of me. Really stupid, I know. But you're right, I didn't have to take advantage of her at all. Cassie, Tasha's been trying to get with me for years. That's why we were always fighting. She's always wanted me, and although I may have cheated on you a few times, the truth is all I ever wanted is to be with you."

"What do you mean, she's always wanted to get with you?"

"I mean, just look at everything. She's always wanted to be just like you. Everything you do, she does. Everything you have, she wants. She's pushed up on me several times, but I always shot her down. You got pregnant with Mia, and look—three months later she was pregnant by some married dude. It's like she was desperate to keep up with you. Your dream is to be a singer, and suddenly it's her dream too. She can't even sing, Cassie! That's why we fought so much back then. You wanted your best friend in Indigo and I just didn't think she was good enough, but because I loved you, I agreed to have her in the group. I even bet if she can't have the man you're with, she always settles for their best friend, huh?"

I thought about her and Payton's friend Damon hooking up. Brice was starting to make sense.

"I never realized all this," I admitted. "So what

really happened?" I asked, not sure if I really wanted to know.

"I just don't want you to think I'm this heartless dude. I . . . well, you know how I feel about you. I'm not going to keep talking your ear off about that. But remember the night when I got that call at your house and you went off on me, told me we no longer had a chance to be together?"

"Oh, no, this was recently that you two slept together?" I squealed.

"Well, I was feeling like I really blew it. I was feeling really vulnerable, Cassie. I called Tasha to vent and she invited me over. One thing led to another . . . but, I swear, the next day I felt like it was the worst thing I'd ever done and I never even wanted her like that. I'm sorry."

"I accept your apology," I replied dryly. My head was throbbing, though.

"Then she started harassing me. Telling me that we had to tell you. I agreed that you should've known, but I had a feeling that she only wanted to tell you because she wanted to hurt you. Rub her victory in your face, but all under the guise that she was so sorry. But I guess when she saw you faint from the news, she knew that she had to come up with something good to remove herself from any guilt."

"Wow. That would make sense. Damn, this is all hard to swallow."

It all made sense that she was recently being so

negative about him and coming up with that crazy idea to write a tell-all book.

"I know what we had is finally gone, but I just want us to be the best parents possible to that little girl, OK? Can we still be friends?"

"Friends, Brice? Besides you and Tasha both betraying me, I've heard 'Shy Girl' on the radio about a million times in the last two days. Were you going to say anything about that?"

"What about it? You know I been doing this music thing for a while. Told you I wasn't gonna stop until I reached the top. I have the number one single in the country right now," he boasted, totally not acknowledging the fact that I'd written the song.

"No, *I* have the number one single in the country right now, Brice. You didn't ask me to use that song."

"Whoa, whoa. That's not your song. We cowrote almost everything back then."

Obviously, he was delirious.

"No, I wrote that song!" I screamed.

I grabbed the bouquet of flowers and launched them into the trash.

"Cassie, Indigo wrote that song. And I own the copyright to everything that Indigo produced."

"You do?"

"I thought you knew this? But anyways, remember, you brought the song to me and I came up with a hook that you liked better and we used my version?"

I did remember that, but I still felt it was my

song, and just because he added the chorus didn't make it his.

"Well, Brice, I just lost my job and spent half of my savings at Costco, and I think I deserve to be making some of that money. Even if we cowrote the song, I could be making money off it too."

"You lost your job?" he said, sounding sincere. "Well, look, I'm sorry for the confusion on 'Shy Girl,' but I will make it up to you. My album comes out in two months. Can you write me another banger? Maybe it can be my second single and I can definitely recommend you to other artists. You can make more money than you ever imagined being a songwriter. And you'll have all the flexibility you need to do things with Mia. What do you think?"

"Are you serious? Don't play with me!"

"Of course I'm serious. C'mon, girl, you know I got mad love for you, no matter what."

We hung up shortly thereafter and I was floating on a natural high. Maybe I'd never be the next Mariah Carey, but if I got into the business as a songwriter, that's definitely the next best thing.

Chapter 39

Payton

Damon called me later on Monday evening to let me know the funeral was scheduled for Wednesday, at 8:00 A.M., at the Downer Funeral Home on Stillwater Avenue. That night I drank a fifth of Hennessy straight from the bottle and passed out. Woke up Tuesday morning facedown on the floor in the middle of Alana's bedroom. Neck and back were stiff as hell from lying on the hardwood all night.

Stood up. No balance. Stumbled over and fell into her desk. Ceramic lamp crashed on top of my head, hit the floor and shattered into large, jagged pieces. The aroma of suicide crept into my senses and took over. I grabbed one of the thick pieces of ceramic with so much force that blood poured out of my hand, dripping onto the floor. The pain hurt so good.

I envisioned stabbing myself in the neck, the blood squirting out like water from a Super Soaker. Like in the movies. Then I couldn't feel anymore. Didn't want to feel the pain anymore.

Life was now unbearable. Death was easy. Didn't have to feel. Hypnotized by the dripping blood, I couldn't feel the piece of lamp digging deeper into my hand.

The doorbell rang.

I didn't want to see anyone, so I ignored it. The dog next door began barking. Looking toward the window, I wondered if he sensed what I was planning. Could he smell the enticing aroma of death too?

The doorbell rang again, followed by a stern knock. Heard my alarm sounding from my bedroom. It was time to get up for work, huh? The thought giving me a little laugh. Suddenly I realized that the sharp ceramic wouldn't cut my neck deep enough. I'd have to use a different method.

The kitchen seemed like the perfect place to find a variety of weapons to use against myself.

Walking by the door, I heard the knock again. I'd forgotten *that* quickly that someone was out there. I was focused on getting to that kitchen.

"Mr. Harris? Is that you?" I heard Pete, our mailman, through the door. "I hear you moving around in there."

"What do you want?" I grumbled, moving closer to the door.

"I have something I think you should see!" he yelled frantically.

Unaffected by his anxiousness, I slowly opened the door. His expression didn't hide the fact that he thought I looked like shit on toast.

His eyes hit the floor. "Look, I heard what happened. You know I been knowing you and Alana for the longest. I am sorry you have to be going through this," he offered.

"Thanks, Pete. But what did you want?"

"Well, knowing what done happened to Alana, I was delivering this package here and thought it was a little strange, considering. Just thought I'd hand-deliver it, instead of leaving it out here. I know in your state of mind you might not want to be checking the mail no time soon, ya know?"

"Thanks, Pete. 'Preciate it."

I closed the door quickly. Turned around and dropped the package to the floor. Then I picked it right back up. Blinked my eyes three or four times. Handwritten with purple ink the envelope was addressed to:

Sugar's Daddy
18 Castor Street
Stamford, CT 06902

In the same purple ink the return address read:

Alana Harris
18 Castor Street
Stamford, CT 06902

I ripped the package open to reveal an unlabeled DVD.

Immediately I realized that her suicide was not a spontaneous rush of emotions that drew her to the window. This was calculated. She wore all black that morning. Mailed me the package. It was all planned. Had to see what was on the DVD.

The image that appeared before me was not my daughter. Looked a lot like her. Same amber eyes and golden hair, but there was pure evil behind the eyes that peered at me from the screen. Her hands and forearms were covered in blood. She was panting. There were tiny splatters of blood across the bridge of her nose.

The guttural voice that came from her mouth was not hers. Not my Sugar's.

"Hi, Daddy," she said, smiling brightly. I caught a glimpse of my daughter shine through that smile. Then she was gone, the evil imposter coming right back with a grimace.

I immediately felt weak. Needed to sit. Head was pounding. Slumped over on my love seat, I stared at the vision before me.

"What should I start with, hmmm?" She was sitting on a crate against a white wall. I couldn't tell where she was when she recorded the video.

"I guess I should start with this," she said as she lifted a blood-soaked kitten up to the camera.

"Yes, yes, it was me that sliced up the innocent little kitty to scare your bald-headed girlfriend."

Vomit rose from my throat and catapulted from my mouth on the floor before me. I couldn't believe what I was hearing.

"And yes—it was me calling her. Leaving her notes. I hated her. Why her?"

I wiped my mouth with my sleeve but didn't

clean up the throw-up. My eyes were glued on the TV.

Alana twirled the knife around in her fingers and accidently cut herself.

"Fuck!" she screamed. "Dumb fucking cat," she spat, kicking it out of view.

"Anyways, so I guess if you're watching this, then everything went as planned. I'm gone. Can't face the rejection anymore. I don't do well with rejection. But you wouldn't know anything about that, because you are always the one doing the rejection. Right, Daddy? I'm glad I'm gone, though, so don't be sad, OK? I was tired of living a life where everybody thought I was crazy and nobody wanted me. No one.

"And yes, I vandalized your car too. I borrowed one of my friend's cars to do that. I would tell them I had something important to do. Like I said, I don't do well with rejection. Thought it was funny as hell that you thought Summer was doing all that shit," she said, followed by a ferocious laugh.

"Parker . . . ," she said, turning from evil to looking vulnerable. Scared. "Parker . . . doesn't exist. Well, he does, but Parker isn't his real name. There are people in this world that you aren't supposed to love. I don't mean *love,* I mean *love-love.* I know that, but it didn't stop me from loving him. I just couldn't understand why he couldn't see me in the same light I saw him. I was nothing more than a little girl to him. No matter how much I tried, he was always interested in someone else. I even went on the pill for him, hoping that one day I would really need them. One day I pinched my neck so hard to look like a hickey in the hopes that it would make him jealous . . . but it didn't."

She paused and began sobbing.

With quivering lips she continued.

"Always someone else. Who is Parker? I'm sure you're wondering. Daddy, Parker's real name is Payton. He's you. You're him," she said, with a shrug. "So you see why I had to remove myself from this world now, right?"

I stood up. My heart palpitated as it fell to my stomach.

Alana stood up from the crate and reached to turn off the video camera.

"Oh, yeah!" she said excitedly. "I'm EvenSweeter too. Get it . . . Sugar . . . EvenSweeter?"

I turned off the TV. Numb, I curled up on the love seat, hooked my hand over the armrest and watched in a daze as the blood lazily dripped off my hands into a pool on the floor.

Chapter 40

Cassie

Wednesday morning came with dense thunderstorms. The humid air made Mia and I sluggishly move around the house as we got dressed for Alana's funeral. As if going to a child's funeral wasn't depressing enough, the thunder crashing through the sky sent subtle death threats to all within earshot.

Damon wanted everyone to wear white, not the customary black, to the funeral. Said it's a summer celebration. She was going to heaven, where there was no such thing as mental illness. There she'd be normal, happy, at peace.

I dressed Mia in a knee-length white taffeta dress, white dress socks and white patent leather Mary Janes. At the end of her cornrows I placed white ribbons.

"I feel like a flower girl, Mommy," she said, smiling brightly.

Surprisingly, it wasn't hard explaining death to a five-year-old. She pretty much took everything I said at face value. Damon said it would be a closed casket because of the extensive damage done to her face on impact with the ground, so I thought it wouldn't be too explicit for Mia.

"We're going to say good-bye to someone who was very, very sick. A lot of people are going to be crying because they're sad that she is going away. They're going to miss her."

"Well, where's she going?" she asked.

"Heaven. And heaven is really far away."

"Mommy, are you going to get really sick and go to heaven one day?" she inquired, with wide eyes.

I couldn't . . . just couldn't. So I lied. "No, honey. I'm not going anywhere."

"Good," she said. All was well in her world. Conversation over.

I threw on a long white linen dress and accessorized in gold jewelry.

When Damon told me the date of Alana's funeral, I immediately rescheduled my LEEP for later on in the week. I wanted to leave my whole day open to be with Payton, if he needed me.

I hadn't spoken to Payton since the Sunday when I left his house. I wanted to call him to see how he was getting by, but I knew that people need their space at times like this. I was looking forward to seeing him, even in the worst of situations. I missed him.

I hummed the melody to "Angelic," a ballad I wrote for Alana, as Mia and I ducked under my umbrella and power walked to the car. Upon Damon's request I'd sing it at the wake after the pastor said a few words. It had been years since I sang in front of an audience, but I wasn't nervous. Alana deserved a beautiful homecoming and I was flattered to take part in making the day special for her and Payton.

The crowd was slowly starting to trickle in. Damon and Payton sat in the front row, just feet away from the casket. Opposite Damon and Payton was a heavyset woman sitting with a man and two young children. The golden hair gave her identity away as Alana's mother.

Damon spotted Mia and me walking in and motioned for us to come sit with him and Payton. I sat next to Payton and put my hand on his knee.

"Hey," I whispered.

"Hey," he whispered back, giving me a crooked smile.

The pastor led the service with a long prayer emphasizing the importance of family. Treating each other right and appreciating your loved ones like every day could be their last. He then spoke briefly about lil' Alana whom he watched grow up before his eyes on her and Payton's occasional visits to church.

"I would be up here hootin' and hollerin' about the Lord, and that pretty little girl with the fiery hair would stick her fingers in her air and crinkle up her little nose. Guess I was a little too loud for her liking," he joked.

The crowd offered up a weak laugh.

"Payton is a good father and a good man. I

hope you don't mind, Payton, that I tell this story. But I remember he came to me after service one day with a tiny little baby in his arms. She must've been eight or nine months or so. Said to me, 'I don't know what to do with her. I can't raise a little girl. What am I going to do?' I told him that there was no instruction manual on raising babies. Told him to just love her. That's all—just love her. He was scared and lacked the experience to raise a child. But he did it!"

Alana's mother lost it then, breaking into hysterics. She jumped up and down, screaming, "Why?" over and over again. The man she was with pulled her back down to her seat by her shoulders. She cried loudly for the rest of the pastor's sermon.

I tuned her out, convinced she was crying over her own guilt and not the fact that Alana's troubled life ended too soon.

Payton looked at her with disgust and rolled his eyes. I assumed he was thinking exactly what I was thinking about her antics.

Soon the pastor called for me to come to the mic. Instantly I felt a rush of adrenaline bolt through my body.

As I found my way to the podium, the music came drifting from the organ.

Closed my eyes, didn't look out to the crowd. Rocked back and forth to the melody. The words flowed out effortlessly.

Finished the first verse before opening my eyes. There wasn't a dry face anywhere I looked.

Keisha was beside herself. Of course Payton was wiping away tears. Even Damon was unable to hold back.

Finished the song and brought the whole place to their feet with applause. I had stuttered through the final verse as I couldn't hold back my tears any longer either. My eyes locked on Mia's and she just smiled, so ignorant to what was going on around her.

"You sounded pretty, Mommy!" she said excitedly as I took my seat next to her.

"Thank you, baby," I said, rubbing my fingers over her hair.

"Don't cry, OK?" she offered.

The wake ended by 9:30 A.M. Damon got a limo for the family, which sadly consisted of Payton, his mother, who'd flown in from Fort Lauderdale, and Damon.

Everyone else followed, in their own cars, the hearse and limo to the burial ground.

The ride was long, but, thankfully, the storm had passed. By the time we reached the graveyard, the sun was shining.

Payton was approached by many people offering their condolences. His face was devoid of emotion. We saw Damon as soon as we pulled up. Mia announced that she had to use the bathroom and Damon offered to take her.

I let her go with him and walked up to give Paytong a lingering hug.

"I'm glad you're here," he whispered in my ear, not letting me go.

"It's good to see you doing better," I told him.

"Not really," he told me, finally releasing me from his embrace.

Then a woman came walking up from the distance, wearing a short black dress and big black shades. Her short hair was jet black. Her skin a golden bronze. It was clear that she was heading straight toward Payton and hadn't gotten the memo about wearing all white.

"That's Summer," Payton informed me as he saw me staring her way.

"What? You better tell her something, Payton. I have Mia with me. How dare she come to your daughter's funeral? I'm going to respect you. And for Alana's sake, I'm not going to slap that bitch," I yelled.

"Na. It's OK. Don't worry about it."

Summer reached us and took off her glasses. Her eyes were bloodshot.

"I'm so sorry. I—I heard what happened. I know you don't want me here, but I loved her too, despite our rocky relationship."

She looked quizzically at me, then back at Payton.

"It's OK. And actually, I owe you a big apology. I'll talk to you another time, but I know it wasn't you threatening me. Us," he corrected, looking over to me.

"OK. I'll leave now. Just wanted to show my respect."

"No, don't leave," he told her.

"Thank you," she said, walking away to join the crowd gathered around the freshly dug hole.

"What just happened here?" I asked him.

"I'll show you later, OK? It wasn't Summer doing all that crazy stuff, though. You don't have to worry about Mia's and your safety anymore. Trust me."

"I trust you," I said, looking into his eyes.

He stared into mine and I felt a tingling in the pit of my stomach.

"Let's go," he said, grabbing my hand.

We started walking, hand in hand, toward the casket, which was elevated over the hole where it would be buried.

In the distance I heard, "Mommy, Mommy!"

Mia ran to catch up with us and grabbed my hand.

With Payton on my left and Mia on my right, I felt complete for the first time in a long time.

We walked toward the burial site, hand in hand in hand.

Epilogue

It was Dr. Weinstein's last counseling session ever. Given the recent suicide of her favorite patient, Alana Harris, Dr. Weinstein had decided to retire. She didn't feel like a failure—or in any way responsible for the young girl's death—it was just hard to get the image out of her head and she didn't want that to ever happen again. The look in the young girl's father's eyes when he looked away from the window his daughter had jumped from was enough to make a hardened criminal cry.

Mr. Harris, the girl's father, was in her office a few days after Alana's funeral. He wanted to show Dr. Weinstein the graphic video he'd received in the mail. She wasn't sure if she was mentally prepared to see something so awful, but she reasoned it was the least she could do to help him gain closure. *This is my last session ever, so let's just get through it,* she coached herself.

They watched the images together. Mr. Harris was choked up and trying desperately to hold back his tears. Dr. Weinstein was doing the same. In that video Alana was not the wonderful girl she'd gotten to know over many years. Even in her medical mind, there was always that bit of skepticism that nagged her about the validity of mental illness. Skepticism brought on by her naturopathic peers, who sought nonmedical cures for everything, and by society in general.

But the images in this video, which contrasted with what she knew of this young woman, would put any small amount of skepticism to bed. It was frightening how Alana looked and talked in the video. Seriously, she appeared like something out of the movie *The Exorcist*.

"C'mon, Dr. Weinstein, how can I not feel guilty about this? How could she think she was in love with me?"

Dr. Weinstein agreed that it was indeed a very strange thing, and unsettling in many ways, but she wanted to offer the proper explanation to Mr. Harris.

"Have you ever heard of the Oedipus complex, where sons fall in love with their mothers and develop a hatred toward their fathers— almost like jealousy? Alana seemed to have developed something similar to this.

"Although, in this case it's referred to as the Electra complex. The roles are reversed and she truly thought she was in love with you."

"But how am I supposed to get past the fact that my daughter basically killed herself because she could never have me as a lover?"

"I would try not to take it so personally. Alana had a very strong love and respect for you as her father that raised her. Since she'd stopped taking her medication, she wasn't capable of translating those feelings correctly. It was nothing you did wrong. Or in this case, right—you showed her that you loved her and that's what you were supposed to do.

"Just know that you did the best you could do. And you handled being a single father with a troubled daughter remarkably. Don't ever feel any different."

Dr. Weinstein ejected the DVD out of the player.

"Neither of us needs to see this ever again. Ever. You need to remember her for all the positive she brought into your life. This person on the DVD is not your daughter. It is a representation of the darkest side of mental illness."

The doctor threw the DVD into a metal waste bin, lit a match and tossed it in.

Mr. Harris watched as smoke started to rise from the barrel and exit the window, right over it. The same window his daughter jumped from.

Later that evening, after Mr. Harris left, Dr. Weinstein walked through her cleaned-out office and wondered if she'd ever practice medicine again.